Hotel California

The Illustrated Novel

Brian C Hailes

Written & illustrated by Brian C Hailes.
Edited by Clinton De Young, Rick Bennett, Christie Hailes, Nicholas P Adams, Geoff Shupe, Marc Hunter & Laura Hailes.

Cover & interior artwork © 2023 by Brian C Hailes. Interior layout/design by Epic Edge Publishing.

HOTEL CALIFORNIA: The Illustrated Novel is a work of fiction. All characters are products of the author's imaginations and are not to be construed as real. Where historical figures and places appear, the situations and dialogues concerning them are entirely fictional and are not intended to depict actual events. In all other respects, any similarities to persons living or dead are coincidental.

* Although the underlying story is loosely inspired by the song *Hotel California* by American rock band Eagles, released on December 8, 1976 by Asylum Records, the author has taken special care not to include exact lyrics from the original song. The Fair Use Exception Section 107 of the Copyright Act states that "the fair use of a copyrighted work...for purposes such as...comment...is not an infringement of copyright." Further, the U.S. Copyright Office says "transformative uses are more likely to be considered fair. Transformative uses are those that add something new, with a further purpose or different character, and do not substitute for the original use of the work."

HOTEL CALIFORNIA: The Illustrated Novel

Library of Congress Cataloging-in-Publication Data

p. cm.
Summary:

[1. Fiction. 2. Horror 3. Mystery/Suspense.] I. Title: Hotel California: The Illustrated Novel
II. Hailes, Brian C., ill. III. Title.

Paperback ISBN: 978-1-951374-85-3
Hardback ISBN: 978-1-951374-86-0
Ebook (Kindle): 978-1-951374-87-7

First Edition Printed in 2023 by Epic Edge Publishing
www.epicedgepublishing.com

Printed in the United States of America

10   9   8   7   6   5   4   3   2   1

*For John,
who went too early.*
—B.C. Hailes

Hotel
California
B.C. Hailes

Hotel California

The Illustrated Novel

Brian C Hailes

B.C. HAILES

1

Chapter One

Downtown Los Angeles. 1976. Chevy Lagunas, Ford Mustangs, and Gran Torinos cruise the busy streets amidst 70's style sedans and convertibles. A warm wind sweeps over the town. Groovy music swells and dissipates with the passing vehicles as happy-go-lucky Californians move about their business or pleasure. Mostly pleasure. Elvis Presley, Gibson guitars, surfboards, and bikini clad babes grace local billboards, which pop up between the tall buildings and rows of healthy palms. A sleek black marble skyscraper casts a large shadow over most of the block, emblazoned with a corporate logo and the words "SkyBox Investments & Asset Management Firm." A building that represents 'The Man' in all his self-aggrandizement. An artificial monolith. An idol. A shrine to corporate greed and not-so-well-hidden debauchery. But straight and tall and presently looking its best.

Wendell Meyers, forty-three, a successful but disgruntled asset manager in a gray suit, bursts through the front doors out into the covered entryway, fuming, nearly shaking.

"Damn you people," he mutters, spitting to the curb and throwing back his dark brown locks. He glares back at the tinted doors or rather the suits standing behind them, shaking his head in disgust and a hint of bewilderment before continuing down the sidewalk. It would seem he's entered the anger stage of the Five Stages of Grief, suggesting he's either just been fired or had a significant disagreement with management.

Wendell stalks down the street, trying to contain his inner rage, bumping shoulders with oncoming foot traffic of other suits or tourists, shallowly apologizing for each minor collision but drawing plenty of attention. He wants to be away from it all. Alone. Yet the streets are more crowded than usual. Pretty girls that look like they're on their way to the beach can't even lighten his mood. The tourists have always annoyed the hell out of him, even on a good day. But this isn't a good day.

"Damn cannibals," he mutters, not necessarily at passersby, but at those he left standing and gawking at SkyBox reception. He wants to sulk for a while. He needs to cool down, gather his thoughts, and develop a strategy, a course of action. And for that, he requires his regular spot at the local coffee shop three blocks down and over. He can't get there fast enough. He's on the verge of hyper-ventilating and thinks he might be sick. Did he even eat breakfast? He can't remember; he was up so early.

Johnny's Coffee House & Diner. He's made it just in time. But as he enters, he finds someone sitting in his regular booth. Three someones, to be precise. He doesn't recognize any of them. Tourists, most likely. He doesn't usually come here at this time of day, but still.

"You're in my booth," he says to the strangers as he arrives at their table, knocking over the salt and pepper shakers, spilling some, a little crazy in his eyes.

They all sit back, riled. The clean-cut alpha male of the trio looks up and shakes his head, taken aback. "What the hell?"

Wendell stares him down a moment.

One of the others shoots him a dirty look.

He huffs, then nods, glancing about. "You're right. Yes. There are other booths. Of course. Other seats. Stubborn piece o'—" He locks eyes with the man again, weighing his resolve, then relents, spinning around and plopping down in the next booth, still fuming.

The man utters something inaudible, and the others chuckle under their breath.

Setting his arms out on the table in front of him, Wendell stares ahead, then out the windows at the City of Angels. For the first time since he bought it, his suit feels way too small, too much of his wrists and forearms showing. But why care about his jacket? What was he

going to do?

Usually, the waitress, Fran, would approach with pen and pad at the ready, a heavyset middle-aged woman he knows all too well, but she's swamped attending to other guests.

"Hello, stranger. What'll it be?" she says to someone at the bar.

"Coffee please."

"That it?"

The man nods.

"You got it."

"Everything alright?" Wendell can hear Fran asking him.

Wendell hesitates, glancing back out the window. And then . . . "Yeah." But then he realizes the question was only in his head.

Fran usually sees through his answers. He could imagine her pursing her lips and heading back behind the bar, hands too full to play shrink as she sometimes does.

Wendell people-watches as he attempts to settle his nerves. Some patrons he recognizes. Some he doesn't. The fat man in the white suit and Hawaiian shirt—Terrance, if he remembers correctly—is a regular. The arguably homeless Charles, with his flaky, red skin and camo, who'd relieved him of hundreds in five-dollar bills over the years. The occasional CSU student. The old man with stark white hair and a perma-tan who always sits at the bar and cusses like a sailor—and probably was one at some point—can't remember his name.

And Jeanine; also works down the block. Beautiful, beautiful Jeanine. She was someone Wendell could talk to, even at a time like this.

The coffee shop door opens, the bell dings, and she enters. How could she have known he was here?

"God is gracious," he mutters as she notices him and approaches.

Rather than sitting across from him, she stands by skeptically. "Wendell, what the hell you doin' here at—" She glances at her watch, "—11:27?"

He shakes his head. "You wouldn't believe the greed of these people," he says.

Jeanine sighs, chews her gum a moment, then sits. "What happened?"

"I don't want to talk about it."

"We're already talkin' about it. Somethin's weighin' on ya, you need to talk it out. Get it off your chest."

Wendell gives her a manufactured half grin.

Fran sets down someone else's coffee another booth over.

"Thanks," says an older gentleman.

"Sure thing, honey. And for you, miss?" to the elderly woman right behind Wendell.

"Salad, house dressing," Jeanine says quietly, pretending it's her turn to order, "And a Coke."

The waitress nods after receiving the elderly woman's order, shoots them a look, and leaves without writing anything down.

Jeanine stares at Wendell, her bright red hair catching the window light. He glances up at her intense green eyes. "You look terrible," she says.

Wendell nods.

"So tell me about your bad day," says Jeanine.

After a long pause, "You're aware most of my clients are in the industry."

Jeanine nods. "Music men—bless their hearts."

"Yeah, so, the stations, labels—they got a chicken-and-egg problem when promoting new albums from their artists. Labels need singles to play on the stations to fuel album sales at record stores, but typically radio stations only want to play music that's already in demand. So they start pitchin' the stations—you know, bribes, payola—allowing labels to pay to break new songs and artists."

Jeanine rolls her eyes. "Well hell, everyone knows that's been goin' on."

"Right, yeah, but lately . . ." Wendell drops his head and rubs his temples and eyebrows, ashamed of his involvement in the racket. "It's gotten bad, Jeanine. *Real bad*. Government's failed crackdown attempts have only facilitated to strengthen the layers of middlemen—people call 'em 'The Network'—but we're involved, Jeanine." Wendell's tone reaches a desperate whisper.

"The promoters of 'The Network' operate through more than a dozen businesses. Obviously, SkyBox is one of 'em. We have been managing west coast relations with the stations while allowing plausible deniability for the labels. Regarding independent promotion for records, we're in it at $60 mil a year. I've been workin' with the 'hit men,' Jeanine. Power brokers. Fast money. It's an inside job. I've seen where it's all goin', and I wanted out. I put in my notice weeks ago, told 'em I'm done. But they've been layin' on the pressure, offerin' more money. Just this mornin', they stop me at the door. We have a heated argument. And then come the threats."

"It's like they all changed. Ganged up. Turned into loan sharks or mob bosses or somethin'. I blew up in their faces and stormed out. And here we are. But they won't stop. I can't get out. Or—"

Jeanine draws a long breath, eyebrows raised. She looks around to make sure no one has been eavesdropping.

"Wow, that's a load, Wendell. A real shitstorm."

"Tell me about it."

Jeanine sighs, thinking.

"Crappy thing is, I love the music. Always have. You get involved in the industry, get a look at the dirty underbelly—whether you want to or not—and it taints it, spoils it somehow. I love those people up there. They're my colleagues. But . . . but they're different now. It's a shame."

"Don't let 'The Man' drag you down," Jeanine says, sliding off her seat and nestling in next to Wendell on his side of the booth, rubbing his back. "Tell you what, take a breather. A vacation. A *real* vacation. Yeah, go somewhere new. Get in that old muscle car of yours, and . . . drive."

Wendell grabs a napkin and clears his nose. Jeanine leans away, put off. She massages his neckline.

"Just drive," Wendell repeats under his breath, thinking.

"Yeah, Babe," Jeanine says. "That's it. Get out of town for a while. Clear your head. Leave all them dirtbags with their labels and stations and corruption behind. Just disappear for a while. 'Til it dies down. Blows over."

He wishes it were that simple. "Disappear," he utters.

Jeanine watches him, chewing her gum, noticing he hasn't touched his coffee.

The two stagger out of the coffee shop and saunter down the sidewalk together. Jeanine peels off, letting go of his hand. He doesn't want to see her go.

* * *

A garage door opens, revealing a muscle car hiding under a canvas covering. Wendell walks in slowly but with purpose. It's been some time since he's heard her sing. He circles the vehicle as a drunken man, except he's not drunk. Drunk with anger, perhaps. Confusion. He doesn't know what to do. How to proceed. Move beyond this total screw-up. This epic calamity. Playing his cards right was something he'd never been convicted of. He could lose his profession. End up in jail.

"Ah hell."

He steps up, grabs the canvas, and yanks it off violently to reveal a black Dodge Challenger with two broad racing stripes running down the center. It's in pristine condition, as though it's never been driven. He's only taken it out a handful of times—whenever he's had a girl to impress, an admittedly rare occurrence. He smiles at the cherry red interior, plops himself down in the driver's seat, takes a pause, and then starts her up. The deep gurgling engine comes alive and rumbles into a deafening roar.

2

Chapter Two

The desert. The open road. *Freedom.* Wendell cruises the open highway, oblivious to any speed limit or safety precaution. Rock and roll blares as if filling the entire universe and coaxing him ever on. He can't help but sing along, jam to it hard. Suits be damned! Bad business be damned! Only the beat, the tunes, the cool wind on his face and hair. It feels good. Real good. Almost good enough to make him forget his troubles or past ties to all things unsavory.

Time slows or speeds up; he can't tell. He watches the horizon, which doesn't change. The sparse vegetation. The heat that turns cold. Eventually, the desert highway falls dark. His comfortable seat starts to become uncomfortable. How far has he driven? He checks the gas gauge. Almost empty, but there hasn't been a gas station for miles, at least, not one that he can remember. *No matter*, he thinks to himself. *Something will come up.* Warm smells of cannabis buds, cactus, girls, or who the hell knows rises through the breeze, filling his nostrils. He closes his eyes and drives blind over the infinitely straight road.

He wishes Jeanine had come along. She soothed him, comforted him—at some point in the recent past, quite literally. But she'd since moved on romantically, consigning him to the 'friend zone' . . . *without benefits.* However, right now, he needed a friend. Or a drink. Surely there'd be a bar or a motel or a gas station or—

Something shimmers up ahead at a great distance against the graying blue sky. A tiny light. A single light. Wendell's head pounds. His head grows heavy; his sight is blurry.

He wipes the exhaustion from his eyes to get a better view through the dim night just falling from dusk.

The light, ever so slowly, grows.

It gets bigger, closer. The light turns into several lights, then many. A building appears.

A massive sign takes shape right off the highway, lit with multiple bulbs around its gaudy perimeter, like those advertising Vegas casinos. Its curved lettering resembles the old 'Pink Palace,' the Beverly Hills Hotel back home.

Wendell can barely make out the words "Hotel California."

He passes the sign and immediately sees what it advertises. An oasis in the desert, the only thing around for miles and miles. Like a mirage. As he thinks of it, he hasn't even passed any other traffic for quite some time.

A mirage in time.

Time.

It doesn't seem to matter much here.

There is something strange about the approaching building, something seductive. Yet the hotel itself is rather bland. It is what one would expect a desert hotel to look like. Blocky, simple construction. A modest central tower fourteen floors high with eight-story wings sprawling out at each side. Perfectly manicured grounds and long lines of tall, gently swaying palm trees out front.

Wendell knows he has to stop for the night and rest his eyes. Get a drink. Some food. They may have fuel or be able to point him to the nearest fill-up . . . in the morning. Definitely in the morning.

As he exits the highway, something strange does occur to him: the overwhelming size of the building, which now looms above. Out here, in the middle of nowhere. An island. A gold and neon island in the center of the quiet.

His challenger rolls up to the hotel's entry drive, a finely dressed valet and bellhop suddenly standing in regal poise, waiting to receive . . . *him.* Their noses turned up slightly; their heads tilted back; chests flared with pride. Arms tucked with careful discipline behind them both.

Hotel
California
B.G. NAILES

Wendell pulls up to meet them.

"Good evening, sir," the valet says, coming alive and hurrying to his door, admiring the vehicle. "A warm welcome to you."

The man, oozing politeness, seems too sincere.

"Beautiful car, sir. Allow me to park her for you while you check in."

Wendell sets the car in neutral, pulls the parking brake, and hands the valet his keys. "Take special care. She means a lot to me."

The man nods with a warm grin and steps aside as Wendell reaches into the back seat to grab the one modest bag he packed for the trip.

"Please, allow me," says the bellhop, instantly at Wendell's side, startling him. He's eager to be of use.

Wendell steps back and slowly hands him his bag.

Both men stare back at him, patiently waiting.

"Oh," Wendell says, "right." He reaches into his back pocket for his wallet and pulls out a few bills, pushing them into their ready hands.

"Thank you, sir," both men say in a strange unison, nodding and assuming their respective business. The valet drives off with his car, and the hotel porter scurries to the sidewalk with his bag, calmly waiting for him to enter the building.

"Must not get a lot of business out here, huh?" Wendell asks.

"We stay busy enough," says the bellhop.

Wendell nods, unbelieving. "Sure."

He breathes in the crisp desert air and makes for the doors, anxious for light booze and soft sheets, but stops short of the threshold.

There she stands in the doorway. A woman. A creature that gives *'woman'* it's very definition. She wears a gleaming tasteful lavender dress, elegant and poised, white Italian opera gloves covering her lower arms. She's ready to go out on the town, but there's no town around to go out on. At least, not close by. *Maybe they're hosting a ball inside,* Wendell thinks, *and she's merely taking a breather.*

Wendell uncomfortably swallows when she looks his way.

She stares and beams at him.

He feels underdressed in his old leather jacket and jeans, like he's showing up at a grand ball completely unaware and without an invite. As he gets closer, her smile deepens. "Welcome to the Hotel California." She

gestures inside the exquisitely crafted golden doors.

He nods as he passes her. "Thank you."

"I'm Ava," she says.

Wendell stops and turns back to face her. "Wendell."

"Please let me know if there is anything I can do for you, Wendell," she says with a professional air about her.

His mind wanders directly to inappropriate things, and he hopes it doesn't show on his face. Wendell nods again and forces a quick smile, fighting the urge to look below her eyeline at the plunging cut of her dress. "I will. Thank you . . . *Ava*."

Wendell makes his way to the reception desk. "Here to check in, sir?"

"Uh, yeah."

"Your name, please?

"Wendell. Wendell Meyers."

"Great. We'll get you taken care of."

This place is the utter gateway to hospitality—a beacon of welcoming. Almost too good to be true. And the handsome, clean-shaven, towheaded gentleman at reception with a gold name tag that reads 'Clarence' proves no different. Helpful, efficient. No reservation needed. *Of course*, Wendell thinks, not having yet seen any other guest. "We hope you enjoy your stay," Clarence says. "Pool and jacuzzi are open until midnight, and we hope you will join us for our Continental Breakfast. It is exquisite."

"Thank you, Clarence."

Clarence hands Wendell a room key. Top floor. *Fantastic.*

As Wendell turns toward the ornate and well-designed lobby, Clarence nods at the bellhop, who quickly hefts his bag onward toward the elevator bank. "This way," he says. "Business? Or pleasure?"

Ava stands statuesque just outside the doors, lighting a cigarette and bringing it delicately with two fingers to her lips.

One of the elevator doors opens.

As Wendell follows the bag porter inside, Ava glances back at him from across the lobby and through the glass, something mysterious, guarded in her beautiful auburn eyes. She holds a secret. Wendell gulps again before the doors close.

"Uh, pleasure, I suppose," he finally answers to the bellhop's quick satisfaction.

Something about this place makes Wendell forget all his problems, or at least not care so much about them. It holds a certain exotic quality for a simple hotel in the middle of the western desert. Like Potiphar's wife likely had. Or a black widow spider seducing a mate.

One of the old highway markers outside, designed as a miniature cast iron mission bell and modeled after the bells of the Old Plaza Church in Los Angeles, faintly rings, barely audible through the walls and window glass of the old hotel. Dwelling on the mental snapshot of Ava's alluring gaze, the elevator engages and moves slowly upward as Wendell comes back to his senses. He looks over at the bellhop who stares blankly ahead like a perfectly content zombie. Wendell then looks up at the lighted numbers dancing over a rainbow line from floor to floor, and he thinks to himself, *I may have just wandered into Heaven . . . Or perhaps, the very first level of Hell.*

3

Chapter Three

A storm rolls in, but lucky for newly appointed FBI Special Agent Maggie Lamb, she has already arrived at her destination. The Boeing 747 SP taxies from the runway to the LAX terminal aircraft stand and connects with the gate.

Agent Lamb sits toward the middle of the crowded plane, just over the wing, so she must wait before disembarking with her one small carry-on bag. A few minutes behind schedule, she impatiently moves past slower passengers, speed-walks to baggage claim, yanks her suitcase off the belt, and makes for the pick-up area where her new partner, a more seasoned —which, in the FBI, often meant more jaded—federal agent named Louie Solarin would supposedly be waiting for her.

She'd heard about Solarin from others at the Bureau, but only in passing. He is a family man. Older. Mid-forties. Among the first of African Americans tasked as special agents.

A wave of warm, dry air hits her as she exits the doors and searches for her ride, a few blonde strands escaping her tight updo and blowing in her eyes. Solarin would be in a white unmarked Ford Galaxie 500 sedan, but she sees nothing of the sort among the many picking up and dropping off. "Late," she sighs. "Of course he's late."

A man standing next to her glances her way, obviously overhearing her comment, but she avoids eye contact, and he eventually leaves. She's never felt more single.

After about ten minutes, Solarin pulls up to the curb and promptly exits the driver's seat. He jogs around the car to help her with her bag. "You must be Special Agent Margaret—"

"Maggie," she corrects him, holding up her hand. "Hate it when people call me Margaret."

". . . *Maggie* Lamb." Hearing him say her name makes her sound like the junior partner, a white rookie female detective. He gives her a polite handshake, opens the trunk, and sets her suitcase inside. "Solarin. Louie Solarin."

She nods and, without thinking, watches him, diving into her automatic habit of reading people—or *judging*, she could never be quite sure which. He seems like a man that has something to prove. An over-achiever type, but generally by the book. Perhaps even a bit anal. From his efficient, hurried demeanor, she ascertains he likely feels guilty about constantly working and being away from his wife and kids. Still, she promises herself she won't ever bring it up, a professional courtesy. She sighs.

They both enter the vehicle and drive off into heavy traffic together. "Sorry I'm late," Solarin says. "LA traffic."

"I understand," she replies, staring out the window. The view of palm trees and other tropical plants, quite different from the flora in Atlanta, where she grew up, or more recently, at the academy in Quantico, intrigues her.

"So you were an army MP and recently transferred to the Bureau?" Solarin says.

"That's the word," Lamb replies.

"Four years back, you weren't even allowed in the club. Good thing the old man died and opened the doors, huh?"

"Yeah, screw Hoover."

He chuckles. "You have family? Boyfriend? Significant other?"

Lamb shakes her head. "Fresh off a break-up, and I've sworn off men for the time being."

"Fair enough." His eyes are back on the road. "How was training?"

She wants to tell him that even though she's new at the Bureau, life has seasoned her, but instead answers his question with a question: "Do you genuinely want to know? Or are you just being polite?"

Solarin smirks. "Both."

Lamb exhales sharply. "Training was fine. What do you know about this record industry fracas?"

"Not much for small talk, huh?"

"Waste of time. Did you hear New York organized an undercover task force? I highly doubt ours is the only other west coast assignment."

"You're probably right." Solarin keeps his eyes on the road, which is nearly at a standstill.

"What do you know about the Mafia's involvement in the payola scheme?"

"Not much beyond the fact that they are involved. You read the file?"

She scoffs. "'Course I read the file."

Solarin nods. "Good, your twenty weeks in Virginia weren't a waste."

"No doubt there will be crossover," Lamb says. "Record promoters and mobsters, I mean—?"

"You might be right. But we're not undercover. So we'll take the direct approach, see how many people we can get to lie to us."

They both smile briefly and continue gazing at the sea of traffic. Downtown skyscrapers stand out in the distance through the haze.

After some time, Lamb says, "SkyBox?"

He answers with an affirming look. Where else would they begin their investigation?

Thunder cracks in the distance and a light patter of rain begins to fall.

* * *

The Ford Galaxie pulls up to the curb. Shielding themselves from the rain with the arms of their trench coats, the agents exit and approach the doors to SkyBox Investments & Asset Management.

The dry interior is a welcome respite from the torrential downpour outside. The agents shake off the water and find their composure. Red mahogany and fine woodwork bathe the impressive lobby. *Expensive.* Lamb and Solarin approach reception. A well-postured brunette beams politely at them both. "How may I help you?"

Solarin profers his badge. "Agent Solarin, Agent Lamb, FBI. We

B.C. Hailes

want to speak with your executives, John Whitmore, Kenneth Phillips, or Joseph Gamble. All three, if possible."

"Do you have an appointment?" the receptionist asks.

"Afraid not."

Her stoic expression breaks. "I'm sorry to say they're out of the office for the day, but I'd be happy to schedule a return appointment. I can put you down for …" She quickly consults her schedule sheet. "… a week from Thursday, the thirteenth? Ten a.m.?"

"Excuse me?" Lamb says under her breath, stunned at the woman's nerve. Did the badge mean nothing to her?

Solarin raises a patient hand to cool her off and gently stand her down. "That would be fine," he says calmly. "Thursday, the thirteenth. Ten a.m."

"Great," says the receptionist, staring up at them with unnaturally white teeth. "I've got you down."

Before leaving, Solarin pauses and adds, "I hate to bother, but could you please show us to their offices?"

"Whose offices?"

Solarin grins. "Uh, the executives."

"Oh, I'm afraid that won't be possible."

"The general offices then. Perhaps a brief tour."

"Again, I'm sorry—"

Solarin pulls out a folded warrant and hands it to the woman. "I'm afraid I must insist."

The receptionist swallows uncomfortably and tosses about, now obviously and deliciously out of her comfort zone. Lamb can't help but grin.

"Um, yes," she says, handing it back. "Of course. Wouldn't want to—" She stands and squeezes past the other receptionist, a young man who gives her a *What-do-you-think-you're-doing?* look.

She hesitates a moment, craning her long neck. "Um, right this way."

"Much obliged," Solarin says, stuffing the paper back in his pocket while following her to the elevator bank. Lamb looks around, surveying the premises and passersby. They're primarily uppity business types, but no one she recognizes from the file. Nevertheless, she can't help but wonder how many of them truly know what illegal activities are happening behind the scenes; and to what level. They enter the center of the three elevator doors.

"Second-to-top floor," the receptionist says awkwardly, reaching past Solarin to push the button. The doors close, and the elevator lurches upward.

"Where are the executives?" Solarin asks. "If you don't mind my asking."

The receptionist clears her throat and looks down. "Uh, no, they're uh, they've taken some vacation days." She fidgets.

"All at once?"

"Mm-hmm."

"Got it," Solarin says.

An obvious lie.

They arrive at the 54th floor and exit into a sprawling work area of occupied cubicles, offices, and conference rooms. A typical white-collar working environment for men and women in finance. Nothing suspicious on the surface. However, a closer examination of their books, which the auditors had yet to gain access to and crack, would likely confirm their suspicions. The real question was what the absentee execs hid in their safes—or locked desk drawers.

Lamb looks up toward the ceiling. No cameras.

Shame.

"What's on the top floor?" Solarin asks, ignoring the sidelong stares of the myriad employees. "I noticed 55 isn't labeled on the elevator."

"Oh, that's reserved for the executive offices . . . and the restaurant, of course.

"Can you please take us there?"

"To the restaurant?"

Solarin rolls his eyes. "The offices."

The receptionist swallows. "I'm afraid that area requires special keys."

"Special keys," Solarin repeats. "For real?"

"Uh, yes. I'm sorry. Keys to which the general staff, unfortunately, do not have access."

Solarin stares at the woman. "General staff including . . . *receptionists?*"

She gulps. "I'm afraid so. You'll have to wait until they return."

"That is unfortunate." Solarin straightens up. "We'll need to set up in one of these here conference rooms—interview personnel, look through the books, faxes, phone logs. I suppose we'll start with mid-level managers."

Lamb deflates. All this would take some time. And she didn't exactly take this job to become a low-level auditor.

"Okay, sure." The receptionist nods obediently—the uncomfortable expression still showing—and leads them to one of the smaller unused spaces at a far corner of the floor, framed with glass walls. "Will this work for you?"

Solarin exhales in frustration, again surveying the office space as though he's doing macro recon before plunging into the micro details. He nods politely. "For the time being."

The real work would begin on the thirteenth . . . *a week from Thursday* . . . at ten o' clock. That is unless they could track down John Whitmore, Kenneth Phillips, or Joseph Gamble sooner.

Chapter Four

Wendell burns to get upstairs, but he can't quite fathom why. The elevator isn't moving fast enough. He strangely yearns to see the room; feel the softness of the bedspread, sheets, and pillows; and tour the bedchamber, closets, nooks, and lavatory. An odd desire, to be sure. Or is it more of the hotel he wishes to see? Yes. The bar, the courtyard, ballrooms, pool, spa, and fitness suites—everything. The sprawling grounds and gardens only briefly glimpsed through the dark. But then, that would be it, wouldn't it? Beyond, only a vast span of nothingness. Dirt, sagebrush, dead grass, and burning clay over a seemingly infinite expanse in all directions. In other words, *death*. Here . . . *life*.

Yet his eyelids grow heavy. *A grand tour will have to wait*, he tells himself.

Perhaps it isn't more of the hotel he wishes to see but more of *Ava*, the mysterious woman in the lobby, dressed to the nines and—whether she realizes it or not—her mere presence set and ready to seduce. Equipped for the sole purpose of invading Wendell's thoughts for an unforeseeable period.

Time.

That otherworldly concept doesn't mean much here.

"Time?" the bag porter says. "Why yes." The man looks down at his wristwatch. "It's just a quarter past midnight."

Had Wendell said that out loud? "Right. Thank you," he replies. *How is it already midnight? Dusk fell just before his arrival. Didn't it?* He could have sworn the final vestiges of sunset saw him through the lobby doors just minutes ago. *Does this elevator operate on its own time zone? Or the hotel, for that matter? Or maybe I'm more tired than I thought.*

"I think your watch is broken," he says to the porter, who smiles and nods.

"Thank you. I'll be sure to have it looked at."

Trippy.

Just now, he notices the lovely yet dry notes of elevator music playing softly over the speakers and begins commenting on the mediocre talent behind such recordings. Still, the words just lay there on the floor of his mouth. Such middling, passionless music could drive one mad if set on eternal repeat.

Above the doors, the illuminated 13 goes out, and the 14 comes on. *I didn't think they used 13*, Wendell muses.

The elevator stops with a ding, and the doors slide open to reveal a perfectly ordinary hotel corridor.

Ornate, violet-and-gold patterned carpet; electric fixtures that resemble nineteenth-century gaslights. Framed photos of old Hollywood architecture and lauded actors from the classical days of Tinseltown, like those hanging in the Roosevelt, line the long hallway.

"Here we are," says the bellman, waiting for Wendell to step out first. "After you."

Wendell's legs seem heavier than they should, but he moves away from the elevator bank and follows the attendant on to his assigned room.

"How old is this hotel?" he asks.

"Quite old," says the messenger. "It's had its share of renovations." A sidelong grin.

"Room 1412." The porter steps aside, allowing Wendell to use the skeleton key received at the front desk in the door lock. He inserts the key's golden lead, pushing the levers to their correct heights while the warded section passes uninterrupted, allowing the key to rotate as Wendell jostles it to the side. The door opens, and both men enter.

The porter quickly sets down Wendell's bag and makes himself useful, scurrying about the room, turning on several lights, and closing the shades. "Plenty of room."

"Hey, how late is the bar—?"

"Two o' clock, sir," says the attendant, suddenly standing before him proudly.

Momentarily taken aback by the attendant's prompt efficiency, Wendell shakes it off and reaches again into his pocket. Wendell tips the man, and the porter promptly exits.

"And what time is breakfa—?"

"Six-thirty to nine-thirty." The man bows sharply and shuts the door.

"Thank you." Wendell stands there a while, alone next to the queen-size bed in that perfect hotel silence one might expect in the middle-of-the-night desert.

He looks around, sighs, and collapses onto the bed, staring up at the white popcorn ceiling.

"Ava," he says, an almost whisper.

He closes his eyes and opens them to Jeanine.

"Where the hell have you been?" she says.

"What do you mean? I've been right here."

"Right here, my ass. I've been waiting for hours."

Wendell tosses about. They're in an old western-style restaurant bar with wood paneling, dim lights, gold accents and too much by way of tacky decor.

"What do you mean, waiting? I just—"

She tilts her head and gives him a look, and he immediately shuts up.

She continues to bore into him with her eyes burning like her hair, so he says, "Sorry."

"You better be." She stands, grabs his hand commandingly, and pulls him to his feet. "Come with me."

He goes willingly, and they pass several occupied tables until he realizes something is off.

Strangers pack the place, but no one is moving or talking. Not even the bartender. As they move past everyone, he notices their drinks have yet to be touched, their plates full.

And then he looks up at their faces.

Blank, pale, expressionless faces, and still as the desert moon, yet they

B.C. HAILES

all seem to face in his direction, whichever way he looks. Their pupilless eyes staring with nothing behind them except pure ambivalence. Eerie tingles course up Wendell's spine as he stares back at them.

"Jeanine, what—?"

"Come on." She pulls harder, yanking almost violently now.

"Jeanine!"

Wendell notices the blood stain on the belly of the bartender's apron. The man with slit wrists. The shriveled old couple in the corner. The pregnant woman holding her belly, painting her chair and the floor under it red. The slouching young man with crimson-stained bullet holes in the chest and shoulder of his dress shirt. The bearded man with bruises covering his body. The girl that looks like she's been in a terrible car accident. The fat, sweaty body missing its head.

Jeanine and Wendell burst through the saloon's back door into blinding white light.

Wendell shoots up from his pillow, gasping, perspiration soaking his back, neck and temples. His arms tremble. He swallows harshly and looks up, down, and sideways.

His hotel room. Empty.

Quiet.

Dark.

Nothing alarming here. Just stillness.

He shakes his head, breathes deep, scoffs, and wipes the sweat from his forehead, the sleep from his eyes.

He rolls off the bed, strips off his clothes from the night before, down to his skivvies, and shuffles into the bathroom. He turns on the faucet, splashes his face, and stares back at himself through the spotless mirror.

He shakes his head again. "Damn."

5

Chapter Five

Having bypassed the elevators, Wendell strolls down an unfamiliar corridor, almost in a trance. He stares glassily at the hallway ahead, trying to decide if he's searching for the stairwell down to the lobby or for other hotel guests he has yet to see. According to his old but expensive wristwatch, it was already 9:34 a.m. when he left his room. Surely there would be others up and about at this hour.

As he vaguely remembers from the night before, the wide hallway boasted classier than usual wallpaper and elegantly patterned carpet. Plenty of room on either side for baggage carts, for lovers to stroll hand-in-hand, or for nowhere-to-be travelers to escape the deep-set cares of the world. Cares like being implicated in illegal activities betwixt record companies, payola, and the mob—plenty of space to ponder one's current predicament or try and forget it altogether.

A hint of cigarette smoke wafts nearby, suggesting someone is close. Wendell straightens and walks with a little more purpose. Finally, he would see at least one other guest staying on the same floor. A strange, inner desire, but one he can't account for.

"Chin up," as his mother used to say. "Chest out. Put on a good impression."

What am I, nine?

Another whiff of smoke, but no smoker to claim it. *Strange.* He does, however, sense a presence nearby. Is someone hiding? Taking a few last puffs with their door cracked before heading into the public area? The smoke trail originates from somewhere around his person.

Wendell squints and follows the imprint. He had smoked a little in his youth up through his twenties but, for his ex-wife's sake, had given it up over a decade ago. Still, he appreciated the hint of second-hand smoke to remind him of the old alluring, albeit abandoned draw.

He comes to a dead end, or rather the far wall of the long arcing hallway, but there's a marked door next to him which leads to the stairwell, so he takes it. Once inside, he notices the aroma of burning tobacco has dwindled. Completely vanished, in fact, along with the presence.

"Hm."

He quickly descends the staircase, passing floor by floor. Eleven, ten, nine . . . still no one. When he arrives at the lobby on the first floor, only slightly winded, he's surprised to see it bustling.

Guests, hotel workers, receptionists, bellhops. A busy morning for a middle-of-nowhere stop-off.

Wendell melds into the small crowd, a new aroma on the air.

Is that coffee, bacon, and eggs?

A tall man with an air of experience bars his way. "May I assist in directing you?"

"Uh," Wendell looks around a moment. "Breakfast."

"Of course. Right this way." The well-dressed man gestures a path through the mass with his hand. He follows it, leading Wendell past large double doors into an adjoining restaurant, a tastefully wood-carved sign above a wide arched portal which reads, "*The Lady & Sons,*" framed by carven magnolias.

A comfortable, dimly lit space, tables, booths, and mostly occupied bar. As several faces turn to see him as he passes, he can't help but be reminded of his excruciating nightmare from his previous dream state and wonders at its meaning, if anything. *Do dreams or nightmares indeed hold actual meaning?* Through the years he could remember, none of his dreams had ever seemed more than psychedelic, nonsensical, and unrelated events that took him through random places, interacting with random characters from his life's journey. Nothing more and nothing less. *So what meaning can I glean from an old saloon full of dead people?*

What must have been the maître d' sees Wendell to a far table in the corner and magically produces a menu from who-knows-where with a quick gesture of his white-gloved hands. "As an aside, the eggs Benedict is to die for. Your waiter will be along shortly." He promptly bows and smirks under a heavy mustache and eyebrows.

They really hire to the clichés at this place, Wendell thinks to himself, eagerly lifting the extensive menu before him.

Before he can read the entrees, another voice turns his attention. "Do you mind if I join you? Unless, of course, you're expecting—"

"No, no," Wendell says, not quite sure how to handle the stranger. "It's fine. I'm not expecting anyone."

"You're sure?"

Wendell smiles, noticing the man's Rodney Dangerfield eyes and spindly, sun-withered arms. "Please."

"Much obliged. I'm Leonard. Leonard Goodman. Friends call me *Leo*."

"Wendell."

He nods and slides into his chair across the cherrywood table, tipping his Panama-style hat. "Pleased to make your acquaintance. I've been waiting for my family to arrive. They were supposed to be here yesterday but got hung up."

"I see," Wendell says. "Sorry." He glances back down at his menu.

"Loners gotta stick together; I suppose," Leonard says. "Anything good?"

Wendell notices Leonard doesn't have a menu, so he offers him his.

"You sure? I'm in no hurry."

"Please."

"Okay, thanks. You know I had the 'Lady's Breakfast Special' yesterday, or was it the 'Son's Pancake Platter?' Days all mesh together, you know?" He chuckles, then coughs.

"Yes they do," Wendell says. "So are you retired?"

"Me? No. Never. I like to keep busy—lots to do. Never gonna put down the plow, you know? Unless I'm travelin', of course. The minute you stop workin' or havin' a purpose, the scythe comes down, know what I'm sayin'?"

Wendell nods.

"'Course I can't do as much as I used to. When I retired from the service, I jumped right into retail, eventually opening up a few of my stores. *Shoes.* Shoes were my thing. If I'm not pushin' or shinin', I'm dancin' in 'em. I can sell anyone a pair of shoes. You can never have enough, you know. Especially if you're a lady, which, of course, you're not."

"Not since last I checked." Both men give a courtesy chuckle.

"And what do you do, *Wendell*, was it?"

"I'm in the music industry."

"Ah," Leonard nods. "I like music. It's a great escape. You play? You in a band or—?"

"No, unfortunately, I'm on the finance side."

"Gotcha. Well, someone's gotta pay for it. I like the instant classics. You know, Creedance, Stones, Zeppelin, Diamond, the ones the moment you hear one of their songs, you know they're gonna be big if they're not already."

"Diamond, as in *Neil* Diamond?"

Leonard grins. "Okay, guilty pleasure on that one, I suppose. He's mostly my wife's. *Sweet Caroline*, I mean, come on."

"If you say so," Wendell relents.

The waiter steps up with a pad in hand. A handsome young man perfectly groomed. His lazy eye catches Wendell's attention, but he forces himself not to stare. "Good morning, and welcome to *The Lady and Sons;* what can I get you, fine gentlemen?"

"I don't know about gentlemen," Leonard says, "but *I'll* have the French toast." He folds up the menu.

"How would you like your eggs, sir?"

"Cooked."

"Yes—"

"Over easy."

"Of course. And to drink?"

"Coffee. Black. And some warm milk on the side, if you don't mind. Helps wash it down. Coat the old pipes."

"Certainly," he says, turning to Wendell.

Wendell breathes deeply. "Guess I'll try the eggs Benedict. Orange juice. Large."

"A house special. Wonderful choice, sir. And the OJ, freshly squeezed. Coming right up." The young man makes a note and hurries off.

"So what was I sayin'?" Leonard starts up again. "You know, there's a pool party later. How long you been here? Seems like every day's Spring Break back there." He motions with his head toward the rear of the hotel. "The dances."

"Oh yeah?"

"Yeah, in-pool bar, the drinks? Women? Beautiful. It's like paradise out there. Reminds me when I was a sailor, and we'd stop off at port. Party doesn't really start up 'til around noon, though, but I'm tellin' ya, you'll wanna stick around."

Wendell sips his ice water and looks about.

Everyone within close proximity seems pleasantly engaged in quiet conversation.

"Sounds like a good time."

Leonard smiles big and snaps his fingers. "That's it."

"'Course I don't know anyone."

"I've made a few friends. I'll introduce ya."

Across the far side of the restaurant, a familiar woman walks in. She's in casual attire; her hair pulled back, a stark contrast to her sparkling evening gown in the lobby the night before, but stunning nonetheless.

Ava.

Wendell stares just enough to tip Leonard off to the object of his captivated gaze.

"Seems you've *already* noticed one of 'em," Leonard says coyly. "But then, who couldn't?"

"Ava," Wendell lets slip.

"Oh, so you've already met. I was under the impression you just got here."

"Last night. Late."

"Well, I was right then. My, you don't waste any time."

Wendell inhales sharply and glances around at the other patrons to evenly distribute his regard and make it seem like Ava isn't the only person holding his attention.

"There are plenty of nice people here if you take the time to get to know them. I find that's true pretty much everywhere."

"Sure," Wendell says, his gaze fluttering past Ava again as she's seated with several other women in a corner booth, laughing and conversing like they're all old friends. Luckily, it's far enough away that she doesn't notice him spying.

"She'll be there," Leonard says.

"What's that?" Wendell shifts in his chair. "Uh, *who* will be *where?*"

"Come on; I wasn't born yesterday. The broad. Pool party. Come on."

Wendell looks down at his lap, places his fine cloth napkin, and fiddles with his silverware as the servers bring their dishes in on steaming platters.

That was fast.

"She is somethin'." Leonard smiles. "Can't beat the service at the Hotel California, eh?" He raises his cup of coffee for a toast.

Wendell grabs his juice, and they clink glasses. "Thanks, Leonard."

"Call me Leo."

R.G. HAILES

$$6$$

Chapter Six

John Whitmore, Kenneth Phillips, and Joseph Gamble eluded Agents Lamb and Solarin during their two-day in-office stint as mere interviewers and technically untrained auditors, which bore little fruit by way of actual damning evidence. Until an anonymous caller led them down the elevator, out of the building, around the block, and to the back of a sidelong alleyway near some dumpsters where Mister Whitmore stares up at them with cold, dead eyes.

Old newspapers, animal feces, used condoms, and other detritus litters the immediate area. The stench of sewer, thick or thin, wafts up here and there from beneath old manhole covers and storm drains. Beyond that, there's a subtle yet palpable feeling that something evil went down here. But Agent Lamb isn't a paranormal investigator or ghost hunter, so she must push such impressions aside to examine only the facts.

Agent Solarin shows a hint of remorse as he looks down at the executive corpse, whereas Agent Lamb expresses nothing. No surprise at the likely silenced gunshot wounds to the chest and temple, the congealed blood pool and spatter around the head and shoulders. No shock at the twisted, splayed-out pose, accentuated by the expensive, now soiled suit. No facial give of pension, grief, or compassion. No. Not from Lamb. This man was a criminal—the white-collared definition of corporate greed and corruption. A monster to all that didn't directly pad his pocketbook. Or his company's.

This was only a fate befitting the wicked.

SkyBox Investments & Asset Management Firm, not always so firmly seated within the music industry, had a history, and not just in newspaper headlines or on the New York Stock Exchange. That history was buried between the entries in ledgers and account books and the standoffish minds (likely hiding behind threats of blackmail or non-disclosure agreements) of many of its employees or former employees.

Lamb and Solarin's conference room interviews yielded little by way of proof, and the cooked books and manipulated paper trail left questionable clues to a racket in payola which was still under investigation at FBI headquarters. But the guilt had been there all along. Lamb had seen it on the interviewees' faces, in their fidgets, ticks, defensiveness, body language, and she heard it in their fluctuating tones. The training at Quantico had done some good, and the *tangible* evidence is somewhere to be sure, waiting to be found, to be *unearthed*.

Now a bit more of it was here, before them, in a grizzly, gruesome testament to collaborative avarice and extortion. And especially now, it is clear that Whitmore wasn't alone in this. Lamb and Solarin need to find this man's secret ledgers if such things exist in the first place (which Lamb is convinced they do) unless, of course, they have already been disposed of.

"Anything stand out to you?" Lamb asks Solarin as she kneels next to the body. With gloved hands, she grabs a pen from inside her coat, checks the breast and jacket pockets, and lifts the gorge and lapel. The inside pocket carries the man's wallet, keys, and a wrapped wad of gum. Money and credit cards are missing. She takes out and flips open an evidence bag, dropping the items and sealing the bag shut.

Solarin, hands on his hips, sighs and studies the layout of the crime scene. "Professional job. Hitman. Double tap. Likely off-site. He probably dropped him here and rolled him out of a trunk from the way he's situated. Near his workplace. Took his cash and cards to make it look like a mugging or robbery."

Solarin turns to examine the asphalt around Whitmore, and Lamb joins in, hoping for some mud or dirt to reveal tire tread impressions or shoeprints. None stand out to the naked eye at first glance, but the CSI team would be along shortly to make a closer sweep. She hands the evidence bag to another nearby officer for processing.

"Professionals," Lamb repeats.

Solarin nods.

"What do we have on the caller?"

"They've traced the number to a public payphone on the Boulevard, but the call wasn't recorded, and they were only on for a few seconds. Not enough time for an active trace or canvas."

"Motives for the tip-off?" Lamb asks herself, but Solarin assumes she's asking him.

"Who knows? Disgruntled employee, maybe. Angry label, musician that didn't get their song on the radio? Could be anything."

Lamb licks and purses her lips, missing Georgia's southern humidity and cleaner skies. This is a far cry from the persona of palm trees, beaches, and Hollywood celebrity residences in the City of Angels. They may as well have been in the seedy, smog-filled centers of Detroit, Chicago, or New York. She breathes deep the polluted air and continues to look around the body, walking slowly.

"See anything to tie it to the mob? Other than the nature of the wounds?"

Solarin takes pause and re-examines the scene. "I just see a dead body."

"Me too," Lamb relents. "Besides, of course, your initial observation that a double tap suggests a pro hit. 'Course, in this situation, a real pro might conceal the fact that they're a pro."

"Sure. So what do we got?"

Lamb muses for a moment. "Pro hit, lackluster driver? Maybe mid-level pros. Does that make them more predictable or less so?"

"Good point," Solarin adds, "However, even dirtbags have family, co-workers, acquaintances, as we've seen . . . Some even have friends."

Lamb scoffs.

"Plenty of people to question . . . if you haven't gotten too sick of the job in your first week. Mafia or not, it's abundantly clear we're dealing with some unsavories. And *dangerous* ones."

But isn't that what she had signed up for? One couldn't make a real difference in the world by tracking down leprechauns, unicorns, and rainbows. Lamb spins on her heal and walks past Solarin toward the car parked at the far end of the alley. "We're just getting started."

Lamb feels Solarin's guarded smile as he scans the sordid place one last time and makes to follow her out.

* * *

Wendell stands in the wide carpeted hallway, a central corridor, an artery, if not the primary route through the Hotel California. He stands there, unsure of himself. Lost, in a way. But how could he be lost near the lobby and right outside the pool area? In fact, just in front of him and to his immediate right, a plaque is mounted to the wall by heavy glass and aureate doors with gold lettering over a sepia finish, which reads: "Pool & Lounge Area." And there is no mistaking the public scent of nearby chlorine, sunscreen, and booze. He knows exactly where he is .. . *geographically.*

Wendell glances down at his watch—12:42 p.m. Time and place accounted for. He supposes the 'why' must have been for sociality, to be present, experience what was being offered, or to answer the invitation of a new friend.

Several other swimsuit clad guests casually walk past him and push through to the balmy outdoor setting. Seems inviting enough, like everything else here.

He appreciates the western desert breeze that blows inside and rustles his unkempt hair.

He's unsure why he hesitates, though the air-conditioning feels nice.

Another older couple passes him to enter the party.

The catchy jam and beat of the music also escape through the doors, and he likes the tune though he doesn't recognize it.

Leo had said it was a 'happenin' place,' and he was right. He had also said *Ava* would be there. That could be the underlying reason for his reluctance, but then, he hadn't felt such equivocation toward a female since those early high school dance days when he was awkward, shy, and plagued with pimples. Now he was a grown man with a clear complexion. What did he have to lose? Besides, of course, his pride? Or dignity?

No time like the present.

Wendell swallows, rubs his sweaty palms over the outside of his trunks, and steps over the threshold. He hopes they will have towels available as he had decided against bringing his own from the room. *Heavy doors indeed*, and he strains slightly to open them.

Pleasantly blinding sunlight dances over the exotic scene as his eyes slowly adjust to take in the azure pools, artificial waterfalls with rock features, perfectly green grass, brightly decorative flora, and sand-colored rock and concrete. Patio tables and gaping striped shade umbrellas stretch over the vast, well-designed lounge area surrounding the water and gardens. An oasis, or desert paradise, to be sure. Caustics of moving light reflect upward onto walking, swimming, sprawled out, or casually conversing persons, all decked out in sparse yet fashionable and party-appropriate beachwear.

Leo wasn't kidding.

Wendell pulls out and slips on some new aviators he had purchased from the gift shop after breakfast, having put up with the ridiculously scratched-up lenses of those tucked in the dashboard of his car for years.

That's better.

"What can I get you?" A mildly attractive waitress in a navy one-piece strolls up beside him, catching him off guard.

"Uh, piña colada, virgin, please."

"I'm sorry, we don't serve virgins here." He wonders if that is inuendo in her eyes or merely her everyday demeanor.

"Oh, well then, uh, water, I suppose."

"Icewater? Sure. We have lemonade. Don't you drink, honey?"

Wendell smiles, slightly embarrassed, not wanting to articulate his opinion that it is still a little early in the day to get hammered. "Trying to cut back. Just water for now. Thank you."

"Got it. Good man."

She lightly pats him on the shoulder with her manicured nails and saunters off to take orders from the next cluster of guests.

Wendell takes to the winding sidewalk ahead, not recognizing anyone in particular as he shuffles along, and why would he? Eavesdropping on conversations of small talk or meaningless social babble, he grows tired of walking around. Eventually, he settles on one of the few empty lawn

B.C. NAILES

chairs just outside the main congregation of partygoers, lifeguards, and employees scattered about the courtyard. Sometimes Wendell just liked to be alone, even in a crowd. And it was easier to do among strangers.

At length, the waitress returns and hands Wendell a fancy off-white tropical cocktail topped with a glossy red cherry, yellow-striped straw, and tipped umbrella. "Just so you know, Wendell, that's a special cocktail. I worked my magic with the barkeep and convinced them to leave out the rum, just for you. Virgin you want? Virgin you shall have. You know, since you're a good man and all." She gives him a wink and goes on her way.

"Thank you," he says when she's likely out of earshot.

Had Wendell even told her his name? *Odd.*

After what feels like an hour of lazy people-watching under the blazing sun, someone he vaguely recognizes walks by in front of him, talking the ear off a suntanned middle-aged woman in a sundress, dark shades, and party hat. Leonard Goodman. The old man sees Wendell and exclaims, "There he is!" He offers the much younger woman a few pleasantries and a compliment, and tells her he'll find her later, then makes his way next to Wendell, plopping himself in the neighboring vacant chair without a thought.

"So glad you came," he says, noticing Wendell's empty cocktail glass on the beverage table and raising an arm to fetch a nearby waiter. "Wasn't sure you would show."

"I've already ordered," Wendell says.

"Yeah, well, I haven't. And you need another." Leo settles into his seat. They look around momentarily before Leo pulls a cigarette and places it between his lips. "Mind if I smoke?"

Wendell shakes his head.

Leo lights up, takes a puff, then points to all the glistening bodies. "What'd I tell ya, huh?"

"It is a party," Wendell says.

"Every day it's like this. I mean, every day I've been here. And I've met some fine people. But you know, I'm waiting for my wife to come. I was expecting her to arrive yesterday."

"Yeah, that's what you said at the restaurant."

"Right. Yes. Well what about *her*?"

"Who?"

"*Who?* Don't give me that. *Her.* You know damn well who I'm talkin' about." He fills his lungs with another pacifying inhalation.

"Haven't seen her," Wendell says.

"You know, come to think of it, neither have I." Leo peers around, obviously in search of the magnificent Ava. "Told you I'd introduce you to some people, and I'm a man of my word."

It was almost a relief Wendell hadn't seen her. Perhaps now he could actually lie back and relax, though he doesn't want to stay too long for fear of a sunburn in this heat.

He does decide to lie back as Leo says something about parking in driveways and driving on parkways, the bright white light of the sun forcing his eyes shut. Wendell enjoys the soothing beat of the music. The light conversational white noise, the tropical ambiance. The natural warmth on his skin.

He supposes that it could have been any season, any time of the year, in this desert climate. It could be Christmas, and it would still feel just like this.

"I knew I could find her here," Leo suddenly bursts out.

Wendell sits up, awkwardly removing his shades.

A beautiful woman with a handsome young man on each arm approaches, and Leo tips the rim of his Panama at Wendell. "Eh?" This wasn't just *any* beautiful woman en route.

"Ava," Wendell gulps under his breath, replaces his shades, and leans back, pretending not to notice her.

Leo chuckles at the adolescent reaction. "Ava! Ava, my dear." The old man clumsily makes it to his tired feet to greet her warmly. "I knew I could find you out here, try and hide as you will. You're looking stunning as ever!"

Indeed, she is. Wendell can't help but glance up at her. A retro floral string bikini with a complimentary sarong and crochet raffia hat. No one could have pulled it off better. Based solely on her dazzling good looks, Wendell had at once guessed her to be highly materialistic but looks aren't everything.

"Leo, you old goat. It's great to see you. Has your family arrived?"

She urges her masculine arm candy onward over the patio, and they walk past Wendell with a synchronized grin toward one another, their chiseled, honey-tan physiques gleaming under the blue sky. "I'll catch up to you guys," she says, noticing Wendell then smiling back at the old man.

Leo brings her in for a fatherly hug, dodging the rim of her floppy hat, which she secures with one arm, intoxicatingly laughing as she goes.

"Not yet, I'm afraid," Leo answers. "Just me today."

"I see. So sorry. She'll come."

"Yes. Oh, before I forget, let me introduce you to my friend here. Wendell is his name. We met over breakfast this very morning."

Wendell heaves himself forward off the lawn chair a little too eagerly but finds composure on his feet. "I believe we've already met," he and Ava say simultaneously.

She feigns a blush.

"*Ava*, was it?"

She nods and smiles, taking Wendell delicately by the hand. "Leo, always lovely to see you, but I have to borrow your friend for a dance."

"Take him away. I need to find me some alcohol besides."

"I'm sorry?" Wendell says to her, confused. "But no one's dancing."

"Not here," Ava says, tightening her grip and yanking him away from his perfectly comfortable lawn chair. "You have to follow the music."

And before he knows it, he's on the other end of the garden courtyard dancing with the most beautiful girl he's ever seen. They get close; her breasts pressed softly and sweetly against his chest. They dance amid only four other couples, but none of them could be feeling what he feels right now. He can hardly bring himself to look into her eyes. Those infinite eyes.

Wendell surmises he's the only one of the group on the pool patio turned dancefloor, not utterly plastered, which sentiment he would like to owe to his piss-poor dancing in front of the only one that presently matters. Whether or not her mind is Tiffany-twisted, in this very moment, he doesn't care. Vanity be damned, but there is something deeper to this woman. She's unique, and they have a connection. And he wants more than anything for that connection to last.

Her scent is like strawberry-sweetened lavender, her bare arms and thighs smooth and sweaty. The heat rising between them is palpable.

"I've got a Mercedes Benz, you know," she says in her high-toned singsong voice.

"And what does that tell me about you?" Wendell asks.

"That I like nice things."

Wendell nods and grins. "I can be nice."

"I bet you can." She snuggles even closer to him. "And so can I."

"You like muscle cars?" he says after some pause. "I drive a Challenger."

"Ooh, challenge accepted," she says in a sultry whisper.

How did he get here? This sort of thing doesn't happen to Wendell. This sort of thing doesn't happen to anyone. He knows he must awake. Was this a dream to balance out his nightmare with Jeanine? He has to open his eyes to that popcorn ceiling in his room. And soon. Return to Earth. The atmosphere. The worry. The heartache. The suffering.

Magical moments like these couldn't ever last, and he felt almost guilty with every beat for even having them. Life is loss, and loss is constant. From the moment we're born, we die, and in the moments where we truly live, we lose.

Wendell clears his throat. "Those boys you were with just now, they're uh . . . *pretty*." He attempts and fails miserably at concealing the jealousy in his tone, as though he has already lost her.

She lowers her head onto his shoulder. "They are. They're . . . *friends*. You'll make a lot of good friends here."

"That's what Leo tells me."

"It's sweet, isn't it?" she says.

"What's that?"

"This. The water. The music. The closeness. Summer sweat."

"This isn't real," Wendell says.

"What do you mean?"

Wendell breathes in, then out. "I'll go my way. You'll go yours. We'll never see each other again. So this isn't real."

"Then why come here?" she asks. "Why dance with me?"

They sway together to the soft rhythm of the music as Wendell ponders the question.

"I don't know. To *remember* . . . To *forget*."

7

Chapter Seven

The explosive mixture of phosphorus and chlorate ignites the tip of the matchstick. With a quick flick of her wrist, Ava uses the match to light a candle gently. Then another. The corridor ahead is darker than Wendell remembers ever seeing it, more ominous and uninviting than before. Varying tones of crimson seem to bathe the patterned floor and walls as though they are about to be devoured by hellfire, yet no smoke or fiery light source is present.

Except for Ava's five-candle candelabra, which seems to spur on other faint, nearby lights, which swell then dim as she passes.

The building feels alive under Wendell's feet, giving off the impression of thousands of lithe serpents sliding slowly along just under the carpet and wallpaper all around. The place looks vaguely familiar and, at the same time, feels completely alien. A sound of far-off whispers rises at a great distance. The smell and cold humidity of someplace ancient saturates the air. Like a cave. Or a tomb. As she gazes back in Wendell's direction, the twirl of her hair and the shine of her silken nightgown turns his attention. Her eyes draw him in yet again. Time itself means nothing here.

Ava's gentle, delicate hand reaches up to take his. He's eager enough to react and gives it willingly. Her touch is warm at first, but that warmth eventually abandons them both. Wendell's focus is drawn to the tiny flames she holds out in the lead; she means to show him the way through the darkness. *Utter* darkness. He will go. They will go. *Together.* However, at first, the tiny lights are barely enough to illuminate two steps ahead at once, and their flickering dwindles, like that of an infant campfire with too little kindling and a sabotaging breeze. Soon, they will have to feel their way through the deepening shadows. However, that seems impossible to Wendell, as his legs go numb. Yet they continue to move on their own accord. Like a marathon runner who crosses the threshold of feeling and merely glides along, a floating head over the progressing landscape.

But at least they are not alone. Wendell and Ava. *Ava.*

What a name.

What a girl.

Something is amiss.

Hints of a staircase, barely visible, loom before them. They ascend carefully, Wendell attempting to blink away his blindness as she pulls him along. Upward. Ever upward.

There are landings and switchbacks between each flight of stairs, and Wendell loses track how many floors they've climbed, but he doesn't grow weary, only uneasy. And they move so smoothly along.

"Where are we?" Wendell asks. "What is this place?"

"Shhh," Ava warns. "They can hear you."

"Who?"

She shakes her head. "Don't be afraid."

"I'm not afraid."

They finally reach the top of the stairs. Wendell looks back at the shadowy abyss they've just negotiated. There's nothing to see but blackness below.

The whispers grow louder, but Wendell can't decide if they originate from behind them or in front of them.

"Quickly," Ava says, her nightgown flickering like the robes of an angel caught in a demon's brimstone pit. "We must pick up our pace."

"Why? What is it? Where are we going?"

"You'll see. I just want you to feel welcome."

"Welcome? What are you—See what?"

They continue down the corridor, the candles' wicks desperately clinging to their final flickerings.

Wendell can hear the converging voices, but their message is muffled.

Obscured, perhaps, because they're all speaking at once. But they are all saying the same thing. *What is it?*

Several dozen of the voices begin to coalesce.

"Welcome . . ."

Ava stops in her tracks, the floor and walls still moving around them. The fire dwindles to mere sparks, embers blinking out on blackened wicks. She drops the candelabra, and the carpet catches fire.

This doesn't alarm Wendell because he's busy staring at *her.*

She has both of his hands now tucked into hers. They are cold as ice, and they send a shiver through him.

Her magnificent beauty shows through the tiny, underlit hints of resurrected firelight.

But in the darkness, her complexion—like her fingers—goes cold. Her soft and supple flesh loses blood flow and goes gray. Her auburn eyes—those unbelievable eyes—glaze over and become glassy, ghostly orbs. The skin of her cheeks and jawline vacuum to her skull underneath, and the beauty becomes a nightmare, the stark indigo veins branching over her face just under the now transparent surface.

Wendell peers downward, aghast. Her lush bosoms have drooped under a skeletal ribcage beneath her gown, her hands, a gathering of bones.

"Welcome," she hisses with a struggling voice, the sound like a murder of crows.

He tries to pull away, but her skeletal grip tightens over his hands, and he can't seem to shake her away.

The fire around them becomes a blazing inferno, and her nightgown alights.

The voices become shadowy personages all around them.

Wendell suddenly remembers the party. He remembers the dance. It was such an alluring place . . . because he was with her. And hers was such a lovely face. Such a—

Wendell opens his terror-filled eyes.

He's in bed, but it's not his own. Of course it's not his own, but not even . . .

This is not even his assigned room.

No sparkling popcorn ceiling. King-sized bed rather than a queen.

New silken sheets; softer, smoother. It's no typically-sized living space either, but a honeymoon suite.

She lies next to him. An angel. Still asleep.

This isn't Wendell's room. This is *hers*.

And he begins to remember.

The pools. Leo. Ava. Their dance on the patio. The drinks. *Too many* drinks.

The party.

What a party.

And then . . . her invitation. These things didn't happen. Not in real life.

How could—?

He stares down at her slumbering profile, the morning light glowing through the drapes. Her naked shoulders, long neck, sleek hair, and supple breasts peek out from just under the edge of the sheets.

Wendell draws in a cleansing breath and settles back into bed. He hooks a pillow with his arm and rolls onto his side to face her.

She stirs and smiles at him with sleepy eyes framed by morning curls. "Mmm, you're awake."

"Morning," he says, still unbelieving. Already intoxicated by her presence, he's nearly forgotten the bad dream.

"Good morning," she says at length, calmly stretching.

They kiss and cuddle in the sheets, and Wendell again gets lost in her arms.

* * *

Maggie Lamb was never a real drinker. Some had even accused her of being Mormon, but she didn't mind the atmosphere of a dusky late-night bar to wind down after a hard day's work. Especially on the road. And with work involving the aftermath of brutal murders, a complicated case, and expertly evasive marks. She likes the quiet mood of the place, the character, the tone. She glances around, noticing the exits, the patrons, employees. The bar isn't a total dive, like so many she had grown accustomed to from late college nights at Georgia State. And she found most bartenders to be nothing like those in the movies; they generally left you alone with your thoughts, the best ones almost sensing when you needed a refill, even without a word or raised pointer finger.

She just sips her Sloe Gin Fizz cocktail with lemon, syrup, and club soda, pondering. Solarin had gone home to his family, likely hugging his daughters extra tight, reading them bedtime stories, and tucking them in snugly. He was, after all, that kind of a guy—at least from what she gleaned after only a handful of days on the case. *Lucky family.*

Lamb might have been green to all this, but it reminded her of plenty of cluster foxtrots she had had to deal with in the service. And many of those situations had never been resolved. Only time would tell whether or not they could bring this case to a clean conclusion. Still, early in the game, most of the deck lay face down, yet to be dealt. But she hates thinking about work when she's off. She needs a distraction—something to help her clear her mind and find a fresh start.

Upon entering, she hadn't noticed any eye-catching young men, but now she furtively re-accesses the general state of testosterone present. A jukebox blares in the background, competing with an average amount of laughter, dirty jokes, and small talk. Ceiling fans fight a losing battle against the smoky haze as pool balls strike to split, and darts find their marks in an adjoining room. Maggie half expects to find only hard-looking ex-cons, hoodlums, or bikers among the present candidates to approach, but the place isn't wholly void of nicer-looking men.

She stands and strolls boldly to one such gentleman seated under the muted, corner-mounted television, to which no one pays much attention. Peanut shells litter the floor around the scraggly yet chiseled towheaded man, but there are no cigarette butts to speak of, which she readily appreciates. She arrives at his booth presumptuously, leaning her thighs softly into the table's edge, but the man doesn't immediately make eye contact.

"You expecting someone?" she asks.

The man breathes in slowly, sits back, and raises his gaze to meet her professionally confident eyeline. Mostly confident because whether he rejects her and says yes or tells her he's not expecting anyone and invites her home within the hour, she doesn't care; just asking gives her the distraction she's looking for.

"Uh . . . no," he finally replies. "Do I know you from somewhere?"

She shakes her head. "Maggie." And she sits down across from him.

"Jon." He nods. She can tell he's not drunk, but there is something . . . melancholy about him. He's over-average handsome, takes reasonably good care of himself, is well-manicured, has good teeth, yet he is preoccupied.

"Have you ordered?" he asks.

"Yeah. Left my drink at the bar."

"Would you like another?"

Maggie shakes her head. "No. Thanks."

After a long pause, he asks, "So, what can I do for you . . . Maggie?"

She smiles. "I work for the FBI. Tough case. Long days. Dead ends. I just need—"

"I didn't kill anybody."

"I did. But it's not what you think." She laughs, and he joins in.

"Does your profession usually scare people off?"

"I don't know. I suppose I don't usually lead with it."

"I see. Well, I'm self-employed."

"Okay," Maggie says. "To be honest, I—I just need . . ."

Jon scoffs and looks down at the table. "A distraction."

She looks up, and he seems to understand readily. "What do you have in mind?" she asks.

"It's a big city, and you approached me in a bar," he says, "But I should let you know . . . I don't kiss on the first date."

Maggie smiles again. "Neither do I. And who says this is a date?"

"Interrogation then."

"I'll save that for next time. You know what, I think I will have that other drink."

"Sure thing." He lifts an arm toward the bartender.

"Thank you . . . Jon."

Chapter Eight

"Can't wait to show you my car," Wendell says, admiring the way Ava holds her floppy hat in place despite no wind inside the hotel lobby. She's fashionably dressed in a bold-patterned belly shirt and mid-length pleated vintage skirt, and she glides down the steps next to him like a summertime ballad, her fingers resting loosely in his.

It had been years since Wendell had taken a girl for whom he felt such intensity on a drive in his muscle car to nowhere in particular. This would be a good time. The *best* time. Now he just needed his Challenger, and they would be off on the ride of their lives.

The receptionists nod at them as they approach the high-set desk, each with a similar, curious grin.

"Ah, Mr. Meyers," the taller, thinner one says. "How is your stay?"

"Great. Could you tell me where my car is parked? Or have the valet bring it around for me?"

"Straight away, sir." The receptionist picks up a phone and quickly makes the request before replacing the handset. He raises his pointed chin. "They will have it here for you shortly. You may kindly wait outside."

"Thanks so much." Wendell tightens his grip on Ava's hand and pulls her excitedly toward the gaudy front doors. He tries but can't seem to conceal a broad, toothy grin.

A heavy wall of warm, crisp desert air hits them instantly as they cross the threshold and stand at the curb, not unlike two naïve prom dates in

anticipation of the day's planned and promised events to come.

"What a beautiful day," Ava says in her high singsong voice, peering out at the colorful yet desolate expanse beyond the gorgeously maintained grounds. "I've always loved the look of a cactus plant. Especially the really big ones."

"Is that an inference?" Wendell asks with a concealed grin.

She smiles devilishly.

"I agree with you. There is something about the open desert. Almost as beautiful as the night." Tongue in cheek, Wendell gives her a sidelong glance.

She bumps him playfully with her hips.

Beautiful, that is, minus the nightmare, he figures. But he would keep that thought to himself.

They stand there for some time, breathing in the dry summer air. It's a nice moment that stretches into many. Eventually, Wendell begins to wonder at the lack of activity around them. No valets besides the one fetching his ride, no bellhops, and no other guests coming or leaving.

He thinks it must be because it's a weekday, pondering back on his mental calendar.

"It is a weekday today, right?" he asks Ava.

"Sunday," she says with a quick smile.

But that doesn't feel right. Was it Saturday back at the pool? Of course, a party like that, Saturday would make sense. But when did he check into the place? Was that Friday? When was he at home in the garage? When did he pick up his Challenger? How long had he been on the road before discovering this peculiar oasis halfway between LA and what must have been Vegas? Or was it closer to the border? Further north, perhaps?

He was usually very adept at remembering dates, times, and places. His job required it of him. Perhaps he had become so intoxicated with Ava that such things ceased to matter.

"Hm, Sunday. *The Sabbath,*" he says with deep but sarcastic undertones. "Aren't we naughty, planning a joyride on the *Lord's day?*"

"I figure the Good Lord wants us to be joyful."

"Eat, drink, and be merry?"

"No," Ava corrects him. "*Joyful,* not merry."

"Semantics."

They both chuckle, and she latches more firmly onto his arm.

A desert breeze picks up but doesn't take her oversized hat.

As Wendell thinks of it, why would she wear such a hat while dressing for a drive over the open road? *Some women just can't be helped,* he supposes.

"Speaking of which, are you religious?" Ava asks him.

"Used to be," he says.

"What changed?"

Wendell's demeanor drops to a more severe octave as he thinks of his father, mother, and straightforward upbringing. All those Sunday morning services. At length, he flatly says, "My parents were always so good." He sighs. "*Too* good. I couldn't live up to them."

"Well, that doesn't make much sense," Ava says tactfully. "It's not a competition between parents and children."

"I know that. My brother, sister, the folks always took us to church, but . . ."

"But?" Ava eggs him on.

"I don't know. I guess it didn't take."

"Why not?" Ava asks, like a little child without a filter to stop such personal or invasive questions before they pour out unabated.

Wendell scoffs. "I don't know exactly. I guess I was . . . *bored.*"

"Bored with being a good boy? Bored with being a saint?" Ava teases. "You're not such a bad boy. Except for last night, I suppose."

"Very funny," Wendell says. "It just didn't feel like freedom at first. There were just . . . places I wanted to go. Experiences—things I wanted to do."

They both stand silent and still, pondering.

And then, *"Eat, drink, and be merry,"* she jokes.

Wendell tickles her midsection, and she laughs out loud, buckling over. They play it through like hormonal teenagers flirting at the beach and end in a tight embrace, facing one another, their noses almost touching. They always seemed to end up in each other's arms.

Wendell's smile fades as he turns his attention from her eyes and looks around them. Still, they are alone. "Where is that damn valet?" he utters, anxious to get on with their date.

Ava looks around with him, and they awkwardly separate on the sidewalk. "I don't know. It never takes this long."

Just as he is about to turn back inside, the doors open, and the shorter receptionist appears, but this time without that curious grin. "Ah, Mr. Meyers. I'm afraid the valet is having some trouble starting your car."

"Starting my—the thing was running just fine when I showed up the other night."

"Perhaps it has been sitting too long," the receptionist says.

"Sitting—I've only been here a couple of days! Where is it? Where's the garage?"

"There." The receptionist points west, or at least what Wendell assumes to be west, the direction of the highway from which he originally came. "If you need any tools, we would be happy to—"

"Just . . . let me check," Wendell says, exasperated. "Ava, you can go back inside if you like. This could take a minute."

"Sure, honey. Um, good luck. I'll be in my room."

Wendell nods and storms off toward the parking garage as Ava and the receptionist return through the lobby doors.

Wendell walks briskly around the main building, up and over an asphalt ramp lined on the right with an elevated sidewalk and evenly spaced palm trees. Well-manicured shrubbery and grounds only partly conceal the sprawling pool and cabana area below, where he assumes another happening party will soon be underway. The drive splits into a rooftop parking lot and a lower covered garage where a simple sign hangs over the entry indicating "Valet Parking." He turns toward the left to follow the slope down.

Only about a third of the stalls are occupied, and most of those with lavish sports cars, muscle cars, or high-end sedans. A steely Jaguar and jet-black Ferrari 308 GTS parked near the entrance immediately catch Wendell's eye, and he wonders at the deep pockets that must be staying in some of the more expensive rooms.

Wendell thinks to himself that they pair nicely with the gold Rolexes, Ray Bans, and trophy wives littering the hotel interior and restaurant— trust fund babies, investment bankers, business owners, music producers . . . financiers. Wendell ultimately relents the judgmental thought and supposes himself not too far out of place, given the company.

As he enters the lower level, the lack of adequate lighting quickly becomes apparent; some overhead lights flicker, causing an unsettling strobe effect throughout the dark space.

"Hello?!" Wendell shouts, his voice echoing off the cold concrete walls. "Valet? Hello? I'm looking for my car!"

No one answers, so Wendell moves deeper into the dark, now barely able to tell the make and model of the sparsely parked vehicles. From the glints and subtle reflections over their sleek finishes, they all look to be in pristine order, but many of the car windows' dark tint obnubilates any view inside. These cars belong on a showroom floor, not in an underground hotel parking garage. Had any of these cars even been driven off the factory lot?

An undecipherable whisper draws Wendell's attention behind him, and he spins toward the entrance with a start, but no one is there—or at least not readily visible in the flickers and shadows. As his head turns again, he glimpses someone in the driver's seat of a nearby Ford Mustang—a sickly pale man, balding and aged with skin a translucent green. The ghostly figure, dressed in a stained button-up, grips the steering wheel with one hand and glares back at Wendell through pupilless eyes and with contempt. As Wendell looks again, the driver's seat is empty.

He squeezes his eyes shut and bows his head before shaking off the hallucination.

It's all in my head, he tells himself. *Get a grip.* Like old theaters or opera houses, Wendell assumes most hotels likely have ghosts, but this is the first time he's seen one. Or *thinks* he's seen one.

He moves forward again, searching for his Challenger or a valet to tell him where they parked it. "Hello?!" he calls out. "Valet?!"

Dammit.

Are they hiding? Playing a prank? These overhelpful, puffed-up chutney ferrits.

A hint of movement turns his attention to a Streaker party wagon. This cyan and orange model must have been from one of the conversion-van companies based in the Midwest. Gerring, Inc., from Elkhart, Indiana, if he remembers correctly. Each of its conversion lines had a unique look

B.C. HAILES

and vibe, and the fact that they looked production and were assembled with quality added to the cool factor and desirability. The Streaker was one of the wildest models, and Wendell had seen quite a few pop up around the LA beaches.

This is a nice-looking Beethoven.

Wendell moves closer to the van. It shakes again, this time with a reaching audible moan from inside. Wendell squints as he nears the passenger's side window and peers through. The interior is a mix of gothic and nautical themes, including deep shag carpeting, wood paneling, and a bedroom with porthole windows. And two naked teenagers going at it with vigor. More high-intensity moans, and the van shakes again. Suddenly, distracted by his presence, they both jerk their heads upward to stare Wendell down with white eyes gleaming, no visible pupils in those frosty orbs.

Wendell gasps and fumbles backward, his neck hair standing with static erectness. It's as though he's a cop at a lookout point and interrupted the climax of their deeply private scene. But in their eyes is something worse than guilt, surprise, or passionate dislike. It is blind hatred. Something like a curse. Turning away and breathing deeply, Wendell wants to flee, but something stops him short.

A hunch.

Summoning the courage, he gulps and slowly approaches the passenger's side window again. Now the van is stone-still. He listens. No more young, gasping moans of ecstasy.

Warily, Wendell peers into the back of the van once more.

Shag carpet. Wood paneling. Porthole windows. Even a ratty old blanket. But no ghostly teenagers in the buff glaring at him with those demonic eyes.

Wendell breathes slowly and steps backward, running a shaky hand through his hair. *I am losing my mind.*

"Valet!" he shouts, the echoes bouncing off the concrete walls and shiny cars all around. His echo startles him.

He focuses on his inhales and exhales, as he did as a child, whenever he would get an asthma attack or the occasional burst of social anxiety. He almost wishes for an inhaler, though he hasn't used one in years.

His neck hairs remain unsettled.

Walking faster now, he searches with heightened intent. He tries to ignore the cars that aren't his, fearful of what he might see inside them.

Finally, Wendell comes upon his ride, or the shiny hints of it, as even the strobing flickers have died down to mostly blackness. But there is no mistaking its handsome silhouette. And it, too, sparkles in the subtle far-off traces of daylight creeping even this far into the artificial cavern. It gleams like it has just been detailed and waxed with much care. Even in the dark, Wendell knows what a clean car looks like.

He wants nothing more than to hop inside, turn the key, hear that low, guttural engine purr, and peel out of this underground hell to pick up his new lady and knock her socks off over that long, desert highway.

Soon, he assures himself. *Very soon.*

The lights flicker on again, and a hand grabs his shoulder.

He jumps and curses.

"Sorry!" The voice of a young man. "Sorry. Didn't—"

"Geez!" Wendell seethes.

"Didn't mean to frighten you."

Wendell nods, gathering himself and calming his nerves. "Valet?"

The young man nods.

Wendell glares at the boy. "Some advice?"

"Sure."

"Don't sneak up on people in dark garages."

"Will do, er, I won't." He smiles that same irritating smile the receptionists gave.

"What's wrong with my car?"

"Sorry. Can't seem to get it to start."

"Have you tried—?"

"We've tried everything."

Wendell looks at the boy, only now noticing the fluorescent lights have gone from an eerie strobing to full-on consistency.

Convenient.

What, do the lights only work for certain people?

"Well, maybe not everything," the boy says.

"Have you checked the battery? Plugs? Cables? Alternator? Starter?"

The young man shrugs. "I wouldn't know."

"'Course not."

"There is a mechanic, stops in from time to time. Works at a gas station not fifteen miles up the road. Gus. I think his name is Gus."

"'Course it is."

"He's handy in a tight spot . . . But probably won't be in today."

"Why would he be?" Wendell pops the hood, then makes for the driver's seat. "I can fix my car. Got any tools?"

The young man doesn't answer immediately, so Wendell gives him another glaring look.

He straightens up like he's new at the job. "Oh, uh, yes. The hotel keeps . . . some tools around. I'll see if I can round them up for you."

"That'd be great. Gas station *fifteen* miles, you say?"

"Yes, sir."

Wendell nods. "What about these lights? Will I be working in the dark?"

"I have someone looking into it." That same robotic smile. The boy gestures at the working fluorescents lining the wide, low ceiling. "And it looks like they've fixed it, right?"

Wendell rolls his eyes and turns the key. Not even the click of a dead battery.

Odd.

"Got any jumper cables?" he asks the young man as he makes to leave. "Batteries?"

"Jumper cables, perhaps," he says, "Batteries? Not likely."

The boy stands there with a blank expression, and Wendell stares back at him.

Like talking to a wall that just started high school.

Ghosts or not, damned if I won't fix this thing and get the hell out of here quick as a prostitute at a baptism.

"Tools?!" Wendell says, snapping him out of his polite little trance.

"Yes sir, of course. Right." And the boy shuffles off with his tail between his legs.

* * *

Agent Solarin arrives at the Phillips residence, a sprawling residential estate nestled haughtily among the upper echelons of celebrity mansions and European-style villas in Beverly Hills. An imposing black fence and rock entryway watched by typical stone lion sentinels and state-of-the-art camera surveillance and speaker system temporarily bar his way to the house.

He buzzes in, introduces himself as FBI, and some sort of butler or personal assistant welcomes him and opens the gates. They roll ever-so-slowly as though the estate proprietor has all the time in the world to wait on visitors.

Solarin shakes his head as he parks inside on the long driveway and begins his walk up to the porch.

A taxi squeals to a halt behind him, and Agent Lamb exits the back seat, pays her driver, and runs up a fair distance—barely squeezing past the gates as they close—to meet him.

"Welcome to work," Solarin says. "Late night?"

"Sort of. Sorry for my tardiness."

"So am I."

Lamb gives him a look and waits for her senior partner to knock on the grand front door with its heavy silver knocker. Each knock is loud enough for the neighbors to hear at least two acres away.

No response.

Lamb reaches over and pushes the doorbell.

After some time, a few inner locks are unlatched from the inside, and a brunette with curly hair cracks open the door. After surveying their appearance, she opens it a little further. "Can I help you?"

Lamb recognizes her from previously studied photos in Phillips' file.

"Hello, Ma'am," Solarin says, proffering his badge and credentials. Lamb does the same.

"I'm Agent Solarin with the FBI. This is Agent Lamb. We're looking for your husband, Kenneth Phillips. Is he home?"

Mrs. Phillips takes a half step back. "No."

"How long since he left?"

"I believe he's in New York."

"You believe?"

She drops her mouth slightly with malice in her eyes. "Manhattan."

"We don't have any recent flight records to indicate he—"

"He rarely takes commercial flights."

"Still," Solarin sighs. "Even charter flights keep logs with—"

"What do you want me to say? Last week he came home for an hour, said he was leaving for an important meeting in New York and left. Haven't seen him since. I got after him for always being gone, East coast, Europe, Asia. He never sees the kids. Says he'll make it up when he gets back but never does."

Solarin nods with an empathetic demeanor. "I believe you. May we come inside?"

"I'd rather you not."

"I understand." Solarin pulls a signed search warrant out of his suit coat pocket and hands it to Mrs. Phillips through the cracked-open door, who pretends to read it. Lamb can tell she's on the verge of an emotional break.

"We won't be long," Lamb says.

The woman nods and relents, opening the door for their passage. "Has something happened?" Mrs. Phillips asks.

"Why might you say that?" Solarin says, passing her in the entryway.

"You're here, aren't you?"

Neither Solarin nor Lamb respond. They only wait patiently for her real answer.

"I haven't heard anything."

Solarin uses his gentle therapist voice, the one Lamb had come to recognize anytime he interviewed or interrogated someone delicate, depressed, or extremely angry with them. "Mm-hm. Laws have been broken, Mrs. Phillips. We're just here to make sure your husband's not involved."

"Or that he is," she scoffs.

"We don't rule out any possibilities, Mrs. Phillips," Solarin says. "We just collect evidence and information useful to the case."

"Well, you won't find anything here. Ken never brings his work home. Only the effects of it."

"What do you mean?"

"He's always absent. Somewhere else. Like every other truant, work-obsessed husband, I imagine. What's he done?"

"I'm afraid we can't discuss the case. You'll have to excuse us. Please wait here."

The woman glares at them with suspicion and makes her way to the designer kitchen.

Solarin leads Lamb through the open-concept house and gestures for her to search the upstairs.

Lovely woman.

And a grand manor indeed. A wealthy homestead to keep, what for only rare and occasional visits to immediate family.

Admiring the large, tasteful abstract and landscape paintings covering the walls, Lamb ascends a wide, carpeted, spiraling staircase rising from the far corner of the great room next to the unused fireplace in search of Phillips' home office. She would first attempt to locate and access his files, then make a broader sweep of the other rooms.

Solarin would find what he could from the main and basement bedrooms.

If Kenneth Phillips kept any damning evidence of his business practices or personal dealings in the no longer 'alleged' scheme between his monolithic corporation, the labels, the stations, and very likely, the mob, they would find it even if they had to bring in a team or haul the man's ticker tape, locked safes, dresser drawers, and file cabinets off on a government trailer for deeper inspection.

Phillips' partner at the firm had been brutally murdered and left in an abandoned alleyway by a dumpster. Lamb and Solarin would find out why and by whom.

Lamb turns the knob to his office door and walks inside, switching on the light. She does find his terminal and 300 baud modem, safe, dresser, and file cabinet, but as expected, they are all locked. Lamb would send the terminal to forensics to analyze and have everything opened through the proper procedures, but that would take some time. She keeps searching and finds one drawer that remains open. With gloved hands, she carefully goes through it, but it only contains personal effects, shopping receipts, and photos of their children and family, nothing related to the case.

She sighs, pondering how to get into the more likely places, when a figure appears at the door behind her. *Mrs. Phillips.*

Lamb stands and turns to face the woman, her hand instinctively moving to cover the handle of her gun. "Mrs. Phillips, I thought we asked you to wait downstairs.

Mrs. Phillips clears her throat. "You did. I just wanted to ask you . . ."

"Yes?"

"Does this search involve my husband's involvement in payola?"

Taken aback, Lamb stares at her for a moment.

"What do you know about payola?"

She shakes her head and begins to sob quietly. "Nothing. It's just phone conversations. When he thinks I'm not listening. Some of his business associates I've met at parties."

"What about them?" Lamb asks.

"I know they're in the *music* business. And others that . . ."

"What, Mrs. Phillips? Others that what?"

"Others that seem . . . dangerous."

Lamb takes her hand off her gun and walks across the room to comfort her. "That's good. It's all right. We'll need to bring you into the office for questioning. Okay?"

She wipes some tears and nods. "The truth is," Mrs. Phillips says cagily, "Despite all he's done, I'm worried for his safety. He's still a father, you know. A husband."

"What do you mean?" Lamb asks. "What makes you think he's not safe?"

"I don't know how to explain it. Dreams? Impressions? I keep getting some—*premonition* . . . a *feeling*—that he won't be coming home."

9

Chapter Nine

"This never happens," Wendell mutters, falling back onto his bed, utterly spent, black grease covering his hands like latex gloves and soiling his forehead and clothing. *Battery—No. Plugs—No. Cables, fuel gauge, alternator, transmission, starter—No.* "What the hell could it be?" His mind flips through alternate possibilities as it did back in shop class. Except he hadn't looked inside an auto mechanics manual in years. He never *needed* to. He knows cars like he knows how to balance accounts, illegally or otherwise.

Using borrowed cables to test the battery and starter, then having stolen batteries and starters from other random parked vehicles that weren't locked to test them, the whole exercise turned futile. And even if the engine *had* turned over, not having access to a multimeter made it impossible to test the alternator for continued charging. And then he had to go back and reinstall all those borrowed parts before anyone became the wiser.

Every damn car in the garage can't have a dead battery AND starter! he tells himself. *Not in their immaculate condition!*

Come to think of it, Wendell hadn't seen a single soul enter or exit the garage for the whole long day and night since the valet delivered that sorry set of old rusty tools in a box that must have been ancient.

As well as they keep this place, one would think they could afford to update their decades-old tools and auto equipment—even if they were complimentary to guests in a tight spot.

B.C. Hailes

He would either have to bum a ride, walk, or hitchhike that fifteen miles to the station to see the man the valet called 'Gus.' Wendell surely couldn't ask Ava to give him a ride after all that talk about his hotrod Challenger.

"Hmph, *Challenger.*" Indeed.

Wendell closes his eyes, not to merely rest or meditate, but to keep himself from exploding in an angry outburst of a string of vulgar expletives that would have blasted holes through the ceiling and every wall like the gun battery of a warship. He never let car troubles get the best of him or go un-fixed. He wanted to march down to the lobby this very instant, covered in oil, and shout all the best profanities he could muster at every smarmy member of the hotel staff, then blame it on some undisclosed condition of Tourette syndrome before returning to cool down in a hot shower.

He wouldn't let it get the best of him. He couldn't. He needed to hit the road again. Soon. He starts to feel claustrophobic in this place. Claustrophobic and uneasy. Volatile even.

But then . . . *Ava.* Her perfect, piercing gaze looks back at him innocently through his mind's eye. Wendell doesn't know if he will ever be ready or able to say goodbye to her.

And it only just occurs to Wendell that she has yet to tell him just how long she plans to stay. Or where she intends to go.

"Ava," he whispers, barely audible. "What are you doing here?"

He exhales, the pressure valves finally releasing some of his long-stored steam.

The release. Letting go. Moving on, to . . . *rest.*

"Wake up."

Wendell lifts his head from the white-speckled table and wipes the drool from his mouth. Confused, he peers out the window of Johnny's Coffee House & Diner, immediately recognizing the spot. He looks across the table.

"There you are."

"Jeanine." Beautiful Jeanine.

Wendell shakes his head, rubbing an eye.

"Coffee?" The waitress, Fran, stands next to him. It's as if she's come out of nowhere.

"Uh, no. Thanks."

She sighs with annoyance, flips her pad closed, and tramps off. Usually, she asks if he wants anything else.

The same patrons he recognized before his trip occupy the place: the fat man, Terrance, in the white suit and Hawaiian shirt. The arguably homeless Charles. The CSU students. The old man with stark white hair and perma-tan.

Jeanine stares back at him patiently with that fiery red hair, a blank smile on her face.

The coffee shop door opens with that familiar ding of the bell, and in walks the maître d' from the Hotel California, the same well-mannered man that saw Wendell to his seat at The Lady & Sons breakfast restaurant where he met his friend, Leo.

The tall man in his penguin suit and perfectly shined shoes, back straight, chin up, walks to the bar and stands there like a statue.

"The hell?" Wendell says.

"Wendell," Jeanine says, "Wendell, when will you look at me?"

Wendell peels his eyes off the maître d's black suit and smug eyes and looks at Jeanine.

She doesn't seem herself. Something about her general demeanor. "No saloon full of dead people today?" Wendell blurts out to see what she'll say.

She scrunches her nose and mouth. "Saloon—? The hell you talkin' about?"

"Nevermind."

"Yeah, we gotta get going anyway. Come with me." She slides out of the booth and grabs Wendell's arm, pulling him to his feet."

"Where are we going?"

"We gotta get you dressed and ready."

"Dressed for what?"

"Don't give me that. As if you don't know."

As they exit the diner, Terrance, Charles, the CSU students, and the old man at the bar turn and watch them leave. The maître d', however, doesn't. He continues, fixated on the in-between stainless-steel worktop where the cooks hand off ready trays to the waitress.

Curious.

Out the door they hustle to the familiar streets of Los Angeles.

A morning breeze blows across Wendell's path, alerting him to the fact that the streets are nearly void of people. And cars. There is only a fraction of what he's used to, but they go about their business the same as before.

"Jeanine, ease up your grip. What's going on?"

"You know what's going on."

"I don't!" Wendell stops abruptly and rips his hand out of hers. "Tell me what the hell's going on!"

Several passers-by pause and give him an odd look, but everyone acknowledges the awkward moment.

Wendell purses his lips and steps closer to Jeanine, softening his tone. "Why am I here, Jeanine? Where are you taking me?"

She exhales sharply, looking as though she's stating the obvious. "To get you fitted. You can't go dressed like this. Obviously."

Wendell looks down at his everyday attire. "What's wrong with my suit?"

"You want to impress her, don't you?"

"Her who?"

"Oh, for the love." Jeanine again grabs him by the hand and yanks him to the sidewalk.

A tailor's shop that Wendell had passed hundreds of times over the years, just down the street from SkyBox, welcomes them inside. It's as he might have imagined it, with beige carpet, dark cherrywood finishes, hundreds of men's suits and flashy jackets covering the walls, and dozens of women's dress gowns in pastel lining the back racks.

The tailor, some clichéd character out of a Night Gallery episode, introduces himself and leads them to the back of the store, takes Wendell's measurements, and fits him with a handsome designer tuxedo, bowing to Jeanine's every instruction. Throughout the entire process, Wendell says nothing. He cooperates, only watching Jeanine, who seems perfectly engrossed in the activity, as though she's helping her baby sister pick out a wedding dress.

They leave in a hurry without even paying the tailor.

"What about my clothes?" Wendell says. "And we need to—"

"He owes me a favor," she says as they approach SkyBox.

Several vehicles on the street resemble those from the hotel garage. Or are they the same cars?

A white unmarked Ford Galaxie 500 sedan pulls over to the curb just in front of the firm, and two people quickly exit. They're all business. A well-dressed African American man and a stern-looking young woman with blonde hair look like they could be federal agents of some kind.

A tinge of apprehensiveness turns his eyes away from them as they approach. Wendell tilts his head down as he and Jeanine beat them to the SkyBox entrance.

Feeling silly approaching his workplace wearing a tuxedo, he pushes through the gilded glass doors after Jeanine and steps hesitantly into the familiar lobby.

But once inside, he realizes it isn't the SkyBox reception area. Instead, they stand in a vast ballroom. An exquisite high-ceiling space filled with classy suits, elegant ladies, maroon carpet, breathtaking chandeliers, and classical architectural details boasting endlessly deep pockets.

Wendell gulps and spins back toward the double doors. Still, the LA streets outside have been replaced by that patterned carpet and classy wallpaper—the same carpet and wallpaper that decorates the floor and walls outside his room at the Hotel California.

Jeanine, who was right before him, is nowhere to be seen.

Leonard Goodman, however, sees him from across the packed gathering and approaches in a kitschy white suit, a burst of red over his heart in the form of a red rose boutonnière. "My man!" he says in his typical, over-the-top manner.

"Hello, Leo."

"Back at ya," he purrs. They shake hands. "You look sharp. What do you think?"

"What am I doing here?"

"What are any of us doing here?"

From the slur in the old man's voice, it's clear he's already pished. Wendell pauses and looks down and over at him.

Leo raises his arms to the crowd. "Sharing special moments with these special people."

"I've never been a fan of black-tie affairs."

"Then it's good that you're not wearing a black tie. 'Cause there's gonna be plenty of affairs. Am I right? She's here, you know."

"'Course she is." Wendell looks around with added interest, hoping she's wearing the same low-cut mauve dress she had graced at their first meeting.

"How many of these balls do they have?" Wendell asks.

Leo takes a glass of champagne from the tray of a passing waiter, gulps it down, chuckles, and shakes his head giddily. "Many as you want . . . or *two*, depending on what type of balls you're referring to."

Wendell chuckles at his own unintended joke, and Leo steps forward to take the hand of a gorgeous elderly lady that seems just his flavor yet well out of his league. She smiles and accepts, nonetheless. It simultaneously dawns on Wendell that the old man is married and still waiting for his bride to arrive. He shakes his head. "This place."

Wendell slowly begins to walk amongst the attendees. He vaguely recognizes some from the outdoor pool deck and wild party the previous day. Or was it two days? Their drunkenness had followed them here. Perhaps he needed a drink. But, on the other hand, he may have already downed too many. Why can't he remember? How long has he been here? Has he just arrived? Or would the night soon end?

"Oh. Jeanine." Where had she gone off to? And why was she even here? She had declined his invitation to come. Hadn't she?

The crowd suddenly parts, not unlike the Red Sea, and there she stands on dry ground.

Not Jeanine, but his unexpected angel. The only one that truly matters. "Ava."

"Wendell." Her voice rings so clearly, despite the low murmur of conversation drifting and swirling like cigarette smoke. *Too* clear.

She steps toward him, her gravity taking hold and pulling him in.

As she draws closer, her complexion darkens, as does her hair. Those guarded auburn eyes become a piercing blue, and she transforms in front of him. Before he realizes what's happening, a stunning brunette now stands in Ava's place. Someone he's never met before, and no less attractive than Ava, just . . . different. He tries to respond to her chrysalis magic but can't find words.

The forward beauty takes his hand and leads him through the formal yet casually loose crowd toward the bar near the batwings of the grand hall.

First Jeanine, now . . . "What's your name?"

"You know my name."

"I'm afraid I don't."

"You've been here before."

"Pardon me, but I haven't."

"Don't worry, Wendell. I just want to get you talking."

"Care for a drink?" asks the bartender.

Wendell nods. What else could stop the spinning? "Surprise me." As if anything could after all this.

They sit at the bar, her slender figure like the statue of a Greek Goddess barely hiding under an ivory silken gown. Such delicacy and boldness walking the tightest of ropes.

"So, Wendell."

He makes the mistake of looking directly at her perfectly symmetrical face, instantly under her spell.

"Tell me," She continues, "What does a good time . . . look like . . . for you?"

If she's a prostitute, Wendell thinks, *I hope I never have to see that bill. Had Leo put her up to this?*

"I'm not," she says, reading his thoughts.

"Not what?" Wendell asks, suddenly trying to look unassuming.

"I'm not an escort. That's what you're thinking, right?"

"No," Wendell says, "Of course I wasn't thinking—"

"Good," she says. "I find people that overthink a bore."

"Right. It's just that Ava and I were—"

She leans in. "Ava isn't here. Just me."

Wendell swallows, but whatever's in the back of his throat won't go down.

The bartender delivers a curiously colored drink over a napkin, and Wendell reluctantly picks it up and takes a sip.

"Mm, that's good."

The bartender nods an almost smile and moves on to his next customer.

Wendell looks down at the pineapple orange mixture with an easy kick, sloshes it carefully, and takes another, longer gulp.

"Back to my question," says the brunette, unflinching.

"I'm a simple man," Wendell says. "Good music. Good company. Conversation. Food. Drinks." He takes another long swig and sets down the empty glass. "That's a good time."

She smiles devilishly, and Wendell wonders what wiping the color from her lips would taste like—a dangerous thought.

"I couldn't agree more," she says. "But only a *taste?*"

She moves so close; Wendell can see the subtle texture of pores across her narrow neck. The subtle, fruity aroma of her perfume, as well as her proximity, gives him goosebumps.

Can you read my mind? He muses.

She almost kisses him before gently pulling back.

Wendell can't believe he was able to fight the urge. He cocks his head and glances around, his bowtie feeling tighter around his neck.

"And what scares you?" she says.

"Tell me your name, and I'll tell you what scares me."

She giggles softly.

The bartender sets another drink beside him.

"My name . . ." she looks right through him, ". . . is whatever you want it to be."

Definitely a prostitute.

Wendell clears his throat, turns on his stool, and stands toward the crowd, straightening his tux. "If you'll excuse me."

Wendell makes to leave but stops short. A hush falls over the ballroom as everyone pauses from their drinks and conversation to turn and face Wendell. Shrinking under the utter intimidation of their myriad stares, Wendell gulps, unbelieving.

After a moment, he steps back and re-seats himself beside the nameless brunette, completely nonplussed. A profound feeling of helplessness keeps his spine rigid, his manner hyper-aware. The silence scrapes like needles over every inch of his body. Her gaze, her intoxicating presence, supplanted by the attention of the room, keeps him awkwardly in place and still as death for what seems a long time.

"What now?" Wendell asks in a tone characterized only by this newly constructed and oddly unfathomable cage.

"We commence getting to know one another," she says calmly.

"Fine. You want to know what scares me?"

"Yes."

"For starters . . . *this*."

"This is only a dream," she says. "You can do whatever you want . . . in a dream."

"Is it? Can you?"

She puts a hand on his leg, squeezing gently, then runs it slowly from knee to upper thigh.

Wendell turns back to face her, and everyone else returns to their pleasure. "Still scares me."

"A room full of strangers? Or a strange woman?"

"Both. Is this some sick form of elitist social conditioning? Some twisted construct to produce adrenochrome? Devil worship? Am I to be sacrificed later?"

She giggles again. "It's just me and you, Wendell."

He looks at the mingling mob again. "And everyone else."

"You're adorable."

"Way I see it, our varying life experiences and relationships with certain . . . situations . . . have brought us here. To this very point. I have to say some of those things I'm not so proud of. For many of us, the things we find *scary* are conditioned, meaning we associate a thing with a negative experience. That association lives in our brains and bodies. And right now, mine is screaming at me to get the hell out of here."

"A room full of strangers or a strange woman?" He repeats to himself. "Pick one."

"I'm not that strange, actually," she says. "And we're wasting time. Do you prefer pain? Or pleasure?"

Wendell ponders a moment, throwing back another drink.

She lightly strokes Wendell's chest with her dancing finger. "I find my sensibilities lie . . . somewhere in-between."

E.C. HAILES

The skillful seductress, her close whispers ooze into him like melted caramel. "Oh, the things I'm going to do to you, soon as you let me in."

Was that a thought? Or did she actually say it?

Still, he thinks of Ava.

The brunette moans softly, and her body slithers upward onto her elegant heels. She holds out her easy, manicured hands for him to take.

His gaze passes over those lithe naked thighs peeking from beneath the slit of her dress. Wendell peers up at the ornate ceiling, then down past his knees. It's the baby blue eyes that finish him off. Now he knows he's been drinking too much. "There's something wrong about this place."

R.C. HAILES

Chapter Ten

The scene was horrific. An eight-by-ten-inch black-and-white photo perfectly illustrates the terrible things one person can do to another. Agent Lamb holds the picture and studies it closely. The crime took place in Manhattan, and she nor Solarin could be there in person to survey or canvas the room, so they would have to rely on the NYPD reports and phone calls to New York field officers.

Tortured, cut open, and hung by a necktie from studio apartment rafters, the man in the photo had crossed the wrong mob boss. At least it was evident to Lamb, only because the man in the photo was Kenneth Phillips. Solarin was still verbally undecided on the perpetrator or perpetrators, but Lamb knew his suspicions would eventually lead him there before or after the evidence came in. *If* it ever came in.

Lamb flips to the next photo, the next, and the next. Varying angles of the crime scene, the body, and other shots of rooms display only small or subtle hints of hard-to-see blood stains or spatter in the surrounding interior spaces.

"So it's confirmed then," Lamb says. "John Whitmore, dead in the alley. Kenneth Phillips, New York. That's two for three."

"Yeah." Solarin exhales and peers out toward the span of windows across the floor from inside the largest of the glass-walled SkyBox conference rooms.

"You think it's Gamble? The mob? Labels?"

"Don't know." This was the sternest Lamb had seen Solarin since she had flown in two weeks previous. The more she got to know Agent Solarin, the more she respected him. Despite her own professionalism and detached, objective approach to the job, the current look on his kind, experienced face made her sad.

A snapshot of hopeless empathy.

"These photos came in this morning?" Lamb asks.

Solarin nods.

"When do they think it happened?"

"They pin it on Thursday. Early morning."

"The thirteenth?" Lamb looks around, pondering. "That's—"

"When we were supposed to have met with him," Solarin says, finishing her sentence.

She shakes her head, a few more dots connecting.

"Yep." He puts his hands over his belt underneath his suit jacket. "What a coincidence."

"Guess they had a good excuse for dropping our appointment then."

Solarin gives Lamb a look and she turns away, focusing again on the photos. "So we've got to find Gamble."

"Yep," he breathes in agreement, "We've got to find Gamble."

"So what are we doing back here?" Lamb asks. "We've ripped this place head to toe. Why aren't we working from the LA field office?"

"I want to question some of these people."

"We've already questioned everyone. Some of them twice."

Solarin gives a nod. "I know. I want to question them *again*."

"I see." Lamb sighs, Solarin's sad determination rubbing off on her.

"The cost of getting songs on the radio." Lamb scoffs.

"This isn't that," Solarin says. "This has nothing to do with music on the radio. Only crime. Only greed. Men and women making money. It's about the transactions, you know? The deals. Accounts. Posturing. Threats. All within the dirty underbelly of *whatever* corporation in *whatever* industry. I've seen it for a long time now. And I'm getting tired of all of it. God help these people.

For a moment, Lamb thinks Solarin might announce his two weeks' notice then and there. He *had* been at it a long time.

Whether Gamble was among the culprits as part of the conspiracy, or whether they could find him before he became the third and final corpse outlined in chalk, only time would tell . . . *hopefully.*

Solarin walks toward the glass doors and grabs the handle.

"You want to send local P.D. to tell the wife?" Lamb asks.

Solarin stops, draws a deep breath, and faces her. "No. I think I'll tell her myself. In person."

Lamb nods and looks down at the carpet. "I'll go with you."

Solarin agrees.

"Just let me know when you're ready."

"Will do. For now, while it's fresh, there's a few I want to meet with." Solarin leaves to find his first unwitting candidate to begin the next round of interrogation.

* * *

You judge distance differently when someone alters your means of transportation, especially when that alteration is disagreeable or unwelcome—primarily considering Wendell had never been a walker and certainly no runner. This and other related thoughts repeatedly cross Wendell's balking mind as he treks along the broken pavement at the side of the never-ending roadway. The highway and long desert horizon boil under the reeling sun in the far distance. Only an occasional squawk of a distant blackbird or the tiny scurrying of a lizard over the dirt breaks up the monotony of the journey. His quiet footsteps and the softly blowing breeze play into his ears, barely keeping his feelings of utter isolation about his environment and his growing frustrations regarding his overall situation at bay.

Stuck. He feels stuck.

The dark desert highway had become a blinding, cooking path that seemed not to change at all, no matter how many footfalls Wendell had already taken.

"*Fifteen miles, my ass,*" Wendell mutters under his breath. He takes another small swig of water, which the hotel staff had hesitated to proffer. They relented only at his third and insistent request, arguing that to venture into the vast western desert with naught but a canteen and the clothes on his back might prove a foolish mistake.

"But I was told the station was only fifteen miles up the road. And I'll hitchhike if I have to," Wendell replied.

"That would be ill-advised, Mr. Meyers. And fifteen miles can seem like thirty in the mid-day desert heat."

They had been right about that last bit. And yes, starting the journey pre-crack-of-dawn would have been much wiser, but Wendell had already invested that time making one final effort in the garage to fix his Challenger.

An unsuccessful effort, though no unpleasant encounters with spooks had bothered him this time. Just another failure, like most, if not all of his actions lately. Except, of course, with Ava. She still seemed to fancy him, even if it was only a mild interest or curiosity, which was how Wendell's previously failed relationships had begun. However, she had also tried talking him out of leaving the hotel. She had even offered to drive him to fetch Gus, the mechanic, but Wendell didn't want to burden such an elegant woman with such things or taint their fledgling relationship with his inadequacies. He sees her as simply above such menial errands. He puts her up on some mental pedestal and keeps her there, protected, singular. And he's not sure if it's out of pride, self-preservation, or fear of losing her before he even has her that he does so. Notwithstanding possible misdeeds with nameless brunettes from strange dreams.

So he walks . . . and walks.

The sun grows hotter.

Scant shrubbery dotting the expanse sways only slightly. Wendell's shadow moves along directly underneath him. His forehead, nose, forearms, and the back of his neck burn beneath his sweat.

How are there no cars on this godforsaken highway? Where are all the travelers?

"Surely it's got to be over the next rise," he tells himself, peering through the heat.

He takes another swig of water and realizes it's his last. He shakes the canteen. Yep. *Empty.*

"Fantastic."

He glances up at the harsh sun and keeps walking.

B.C. HAILES

"Come on, Gus." *That wet-nosed valet better not have lied to me,* he thinks. *I'll break his legs with my tailpipe.*

Something shimmers in the distance, catching his sunburned eyes.

The reflection of the sun on the hood or canopy of a vehicle.

Wendell squints, his gaze blurry. Why had he left his shades back at the hotel? Forgetfulness? Too lazy to walk back up to his room to grab them?

It was a car!

Salvation.

Wendell slowly walks into the middle of the road.

Most people avoided hitchhikers, but Wendell wouldn't let this one simply drive past without a fight.

Wendell recognizes the make and model as the car approaches: a Vauxhall Viva. In . . . blue?

Wendell raises his arms and waves at the driver, carefully straddling the dotted yellow line while leaning toward the oncoming traffic at his left.

The faded, cyan-colored car with a white top decelerates and stops just in front of him, and Wendell traipses over to the driver's side window as it rolls down.

"You alright there?" says a burly man in a dirt-stained wife-beater. Someone balding, middle-aged, and overweight with greasy hair never seemed so welcoming.

"Yes, hi, my name's Wendell. And I could use a ride."

"You look it. Where you headed?" asks the man matter-of-factly.

"I'm looking for a gas station."

"I just passed one," he says. "Just a few miles back."

Wendell closes his eyes, exhaling in joyful relief. "I know it's a huge inconvenience, and I hate to ask you to backtrack, but could you take me there? I can pay you. Handsomely. I'm willing to pay you for your time and gas."

The man glances down at his odometer. "There is somewhere I gotta be, but I suppose I can spare a few minutes. Looks like I've got just over a third of a tank, but I guess I could fill up back there. Sure. Hop in."

Wendell exhales deeply and taps the hood of the man's car. "Thanks so much. You're a lifesaver."

"Sure thing." The man flicks some garbage and crumbs off the passenger seat, making space.

Wendell steps around the vehicle and enters, kicking away empty glass bottles and magazines at his feet with a wave of relief. Even just the shade from the sun is a welcome respite, despite the pungent smells of old food, spilled drinks, and potent body odor.

"I'm Lewis." He offers Wendell a hand. "Lewis Mitchell."

They shake.

Lewis turns his car about, one tire leaving the pavement and taking out several small scrub oak plants, and they take off toward the station.

As they drive, Lewis says nothing and watches the road ahead.

"You from around here?" Wendell asks.

"Nah, I'm from Detroit. Ain't nothin' 'round here."

Wendell chuckles. "Isn't that the truth?"

Feeling like he ought to engage Lewis in a cordial bout of get-to-know-you small-talk, Wendell doesn't have the energy, and he presently cares about the man's would-be answers even less.

The Viva hums and rattles over the highway just over the speed limit.

Wendell leans his head back restfully and keeps his eyes peeled for the station.

After an extended pause of silence between the men, the old signpost, faded gas price boards, and station appear afar off.

"There you go," says Lewis. "Thought I saw the place."

"He wasn't lying," Wendell utters, referring to the young valet in the parking garage. However, the closer Wendell looks at the station, the more derelict and abandoned it seems. "That a working station?"

Lewis, too, makes a closer inspection. "I think so . . . maybe."

They pull in and park at one of the two rusty pumps available.

With a heave and a grunt, Lewis exits the small vehicle to pay the attendant and pump the gas himself.

Wendell also steps out and searches for signs of life.

Attached to the station is a two-car mechanics garage, but the ratty doors are closed and locked, windows dark. Wendell follows Lewis inside the station's main entrance.

No one is at the front desk.

Lewis looks over at Wendell. "Maybe it is abandoned. Never seen a gas pump on the honor system."

Wendell doesn't smile. If he has to ask Lewis to return him to the hotel empty-handed, or worse, walk back if Lewis needs to leave and Wendell wants to explore the shop's tool supply further, there'd be hell to pay.

At length, they hear a toilet flush, and an old, withered man in suspenders shuffles out of the single lavatory in the back.

The two watch as the old hunchback attendant takes his sweet time re-manning his post at the cash register. "Which pump?" he asks, glancing out the grimy, obscured window to his left.

"Two," says Lewis.

"Right. How much?"

"Six."

"You want me to pump it for you—?"

"I got it," Lewis says, giving Wendell a look, paying the old man in cash, and pushing back through the front door.

Wendell smiles at Lewis and turns back to face the attendant. "Are you Gus?"

He shakes his head.

"Is he around?"

"As I recall, Gus hasn't worked here for some time now."

"Wait," Wendell says. "What? The folks at the hotel said—"

"Hotel California?"

Wendell takes a pause. "Yeah, they—"

"Look son, don't listen to anything they tell ya down there. They're a bunch o' flee-ridden shit bags in their expensiv—"

"I need a mechanic," Wendell says. "Who runs this shop here?"

"Hm," the old man looks down. "At present? Nobody. I used to, but—"

Wendell notices the man's hands trembling rhythmically and wonders if it was Parkinson's, multiple sclerosis, or liver failure that ended his usefulness in the shop.

"I need some tools, parts. You mind if I—?"

"Borrow?"

Their eyes meet as though the old man is judging whether or not he's a thief.

"Go right ahead. I'll open it up from the back. You'll need to go around."

"Great. Thanks so much. Oh, and a—you got some kind of ride around here?"

"Yeah, sure."

"Thank you." Wendell exits out the front and walks toward Lewis, who's still working the ancient gas pump on two.

Wendell grabs his wallet and hands Lewis a fifty.

"Woah. That's too much," Lewis says. "It was just a couple o' miles."

"Trust me. It's not." Wendell nods. "Thanks again for the ride."

Lewis finishes up and takes the cash. "Any time." He plops himself into the driver's seat and brings the seatbelt snuggly over his wide girth, snapping it in place. "So you all set then? I do have to go."

"Yeah." Wendell taps the canopy of the man's car.

"Good luck." Lewis pulls back out onto the highway and takes off down the road.

"Least crazy person I've met," Wendell whispers to himself. "Despite looking like a serial killer."

Wendell takes a deep breath and walks around to the rear of the garage, passing a broken-down VW Bug. The back door is open, so he enters, expecting to see the old man standing there, ready to show him what's available, but the attendant is nowhere in sight. Wendell makes his way to the cash register, but he's not there either.

"Where'd you go?" Wendell pokes his head into the phonebooth-sized restroom, the shed out back, storage closet, grease pit, AC and generator nook, up and down the three aisles of sparsely stocked shelves of snacks and drinks—grabbing a soda and guzzling it as he searches—then back out to the shop.

No one.

"Where the hell? *Mister*—?!" Why hadn't he asked the man's name? "Mister?! Anyone?!"

Wendell runs back out onto the highway and peers into the distance to see if he can spy Lewis's car, but it has already vanished over the boiling horizon. He chucks the empty soda bottle, shattering it over the pavement.

"Shit."

He looks back at the derelict, abandoned station, his eyes still frantically searching for movement, shadows, or any trace of the old man.

Nothing.

"Dammit!"

GAS

11

Chapter Eleven

No cars parked in the garage. Only broken down, derelict vehicles taken over by weeds or half-buried in windswept desert sands out the back frame the property's perimeter, coalescing into a junkyard of wagon corpses. An eternity of distance and nothingness in all directions, save that damnable hotel to the west. *To the west.* Fifteen-*plus* miles. Even if Wendell did manage to scrounge up a working ride, would he return to the Hotel California? Or go another way? East, perhaps—the only other option with a paved road. East and north and on to Vegas, Searchlight, or Mohave Valley, depending on which highway this happened to be. Wendell can't quite remember, and road signs in this area are scarce. All he can recall is that he's somewhere in California's eastern desert region just north of Mexico, maybe a third of the way between LA and Flagstaff, possibly bordering the Mohave Desert. *Possibly.* He could hit Paradise and Vegas if the highway arced north, connected with I-15. Ah, yes, Vegas. He would have plenty of gas. Lewis had filled up here. *East.* Yes, he would find help in one of those places. He would find civilization—even *salvation.*

But can he leave his Challenger behind in that haunted parking garage for so long unattended? Can he bring himself to abandon Ava? He does have a job to get back to . . . *if it's still there after everything that went down between him and the partners.*

Of course, none of that matters if he can't come up with a set of wheels. Wendell's eyes case the long unused mechanic's shop. Though covered in years of dust, rust, and old oil, plenty of tools are scattered around—tools and machinery for almost any auto-related job. And the place seems to have power, albeit threatening to sputter and shut off at any moment. Wendell's brain rolls back into recall mode. Upon searching the place for not-Gus, he had walked around the west side of the garage at least twice and, in so doing, passed a broken-down VW Bug with flat tires and ratty seats nestled against a wall. It was half-covered with a torn-up tarp that more closely resembled a zombie's parka that had already been through the apocalypse.

"The Bug," he mutters to himself.

Could he get it working? Resurrect the old beater?

He exhales softly and takes one long last look around before moving forward.

Wendell walks to the dusty tool cabinet and rummages through the drawers, searching for his go-to tools. They're old, but they're serviceable.

He takes the wrenches, ratchets, tire irons and a hammer up in a massive bundle under his arms for his first trip around the building and waddles out the back door. Dropping them in the dirt next to the old Bug, he takes his time looking her over.

"Damn, you're in bad shape."

Then he returns inside, hits the head—half expecting to see the old man poke his ghostly bald pate through the door as he sits pondering, grabs another drink, and fetches another big load of tools.

Standing there, he looks the car over once again. "Get to work, Meyers," he utters to himself.

He drops the tools, reaches up, and yanks off the tarp with an explosion of dust and grime.

It had already been a long day. Now it would be an even longer night.

* * *

"Your hunch was right," Solarin says to Agent Lamb. "Mob's involvement is confirmed."

Lamb nods, and they both draw their side arms. She nudges the door open with her foot. It squeaks ajar, and their shadows stretch down the long dark hallway before them.

The Los Angeles field office had let them in on the report. Their counterparts in New York, with the help of the N.Y.P.D., while investigating the murder of Kenneth Phillips, had surveilled reputed Mafia boss Angelo Rossi and three of his top lieutenants in the Gallo family. A camera crew was following Tom De Luca, an LA record promoter who supposedly was meeting the mobsters at the same hotel Phillips was found hanging dead in. When taken together, paper trails, receipts, and witness reports from said camera crew did tie John Whitmore, Kenneth Phillips, and Joseph Gamble to the racket indirectly. And since Phillips and Whitmore were already wiped off the table, that left only Gamble to question. But New York's investigations weren't the only ones yielding results; Solarin, with the help of the crime scene photos and the passage of time, had been able to squeeze considerably more information from not only Gamble's assistant, (who hadn't had much to do at SkyBox with the three executives missing in action for over three weeks) but also Phillips' new widow. Upon hearing of her husband's confirmed death, she opened up with more detail. She cooperated more fully in disclosing the existence of a storage unit, which contained many of Phillips' prized belongings, business reports, and secret ledgers.

And those led agents Lamb and Solarin here, to a new address, just outside Beverly Hills. An off-site office where the executives allegedly conducted some of their *side* business dealings.

An excellent office space, to be sure; however, in light of recent findings, the grisly deaths of two of its previous occupiers, and the fact that it was the middle of the night, a sinister atmosphere hung over and permeated the place.

Training their weapons forward, Lamb and Solarin move through the door and into the long hallway, sweeping nooks and checking side offices, all pitch dark and quiet. They are on the third and top floor of the building, in an upscale part of town, but it doesn't feel that way. Remembering her training, Lamb leads out, followed by Solarin, who has her back. Searching down their sites, they cover every possible space furtively, systematically, eyes wide, and hyper-aware.

Flipping on the lights as they enter and case each of the first five offices, their closets, and lavatories, one by one, until they get to the last, the biggest, the corner office, they take pause at number six.

Gamble had not been seen at home. They could find no travel receipts. No trail, paper or otherwise. Only a handwritten address was scribbled in a page's top corner in one of Phillips' ledgers. *So, unless Gamble's in some late-night bar or lying in a ditch somewhere, he's likely here,* Lamb thinks to herself; Solarin is probably sharing the connected dots.

He opens the door. Lamb enters first, training her handgun between shadows. A tiny fiery light appears; the tip of a lit cigarette. The faint glow of it illuminates the cheeks of a stout, smug face hovering in the blackness. Someone sits at the desk in the center of the room. A man. A very *large* man.

Solarin flips on the blinding lights, and they move in on him at ten and two, leading with their government-issued weapons. Gamble curses at their presence or the bright light hurting his eyes. He is seated squarely at his office desk, one hand on the table and the other fingering his smoke. No papers present. No files on his desk. No computer. The place is clean, as the cleaning ladies likely left it. There was no work being done this night. Not by Gamble. No. He was hiding. Waiting. Lying low. He was merely . . . *here.*

"Joseph Gamble? FBI." Lamb recognizes him from the photos in the reports and on his SkyBox office walls.

"Hands where we can see them," Solarin says, sounding perfectly cliché.

The man doesn't lift his arms, doesn't nod, doesn't cooperate. He just sits there, ignoring them, enjoying his tab from under well-kept stark white hair, that complacent gaze, the typical Rolex and expensive suit for someone of his elitist financial position—obviously, a man of business and a poser that poses well.

Lamb hesitates, intimidated by his commanding presence—that condescending glare behind the billowing smoke. Not to mention he's at least three times her size. She gulps. But Solarin has her back. "You're under arrest." Lamb quickly moves to his side, behind the desk, holsters her weapon, and retrieves the handcuffs from her belt. She grabs one of his massive arms to bring it around, and the man swats it away and slaps her hard to the floor. "Don't touch me, woman! And let me call my lawyer."

He reaches for his phone.

Solarin approaches with vengeance in his eyes, nearly pulling the trigger, the barrel of his gun positioned so Gamble can't focus on anything else. "Don't," Solarin seethes.

"It's alright, I'm alright," Lamb says.

Gamble smiles smugly. "FBI," he utters.

Lamb quickly returns to her feet, ears ringing, her face throbbing with pain.

Gritting her teeth, she grabs his arm again—much more forcefully this time. Then the other. "Stand up!"

The man slowly shakes his head but finally relents.

She cuffs him tight, he winces, and they move him to the door. He takes his time, and there's not much she nor Solarin can do to hurry him along, considering Gamble's utter size.

She wants to say something, read him Miranda rights like in the movies, but those aren't Federal, and they're often provided in writing so a defendant may waive them in writing.

This man would be playing it as expected—from behind a phalanx of counsel. Likely, the best money could buy.

"Are you aware that your partner, John Whitmore, was found dead in an alley here in LA?" Solarin asks. "Or that your other partner, Kenneth Phillips, was murdered in a New York hotel recently? Perhaps it's *our* protection you need."

Gamble ignores the questions as they slowly make their way to the elevators.

Already knowing the answer, Lamb asks, "Were Phillips and Whitmore involved with mob dealings? Payola? What's your stake in it? Did you sell out those closest to you?"

Again, the financial titan neglects their questioning. Lamb knows Solarin doesn't expect him to open his mouth, and neither does she, so it surprises them when they enter the elevator, and he does.

"I am not involved in whatever schemes you speak of," Gamble says coolly, his voice low like the guttural hum of a bison.

"Is that right?" Solarin says. "And I suppose you will enlighten us as to who is responsible for this racket?"

"Hm," Gamble scoffs. "Two men, actually. And I regret to say they were under our employ, my partners and me. We have since let them go."

"Who?" Lamb asks, as if anything the man says can be trusted. Still, it would go on the record.

Gamble clears his throat and glances her way, Lamb noticing how much taller he is than her. "SkyBox's cash manager and their former chief accounting officer."

His phrasing, Lamb notices, attempting to distance himself from the company. His *own* company.

"Their names?" Solarin asks.

Lamb tries unsuccessfully to remember from the documents they poured over for weeks.

The elevator doors close, Solarin hits the button for the lobby, and the elevator lurches downward.

"Let me think," Gamble says, stalling.

"Don't tell me you can't remember the names of your own cash manager and CAO," Lamb says. "Funny how obvious details get foggy when you're under suspicion of murder and indictment for fraud, corruption, and bribery."

"Oh, and don't forget assaulting a federal officer," Solarin adds.

Lamb points at Solarin. "Yes."

Gamble clears his throat again, ignoring the quips. "Jeremey Bianchi and Wendell Meyers. Those are the men you're after. I'm innocent, as my lawyers will soon prove."

"Jeremy Bianchi and Wendell Meyers?" Lamb repeats back. The names sound familiar, but she is reasonably sure those two had also been MIA since the onset of their investigation.

Gamble doesn't respond, so Lamb can only assume she heard him correctly.

The car reaches the main floor, the doors open, and Lamb and Solarin shove the huge man out of the elevator bank.

"Careful," Gamble says, "or I'll sue you for ruining a perfectly fine suit."

* * *

"What was it the writer said? *None are completely wretched except those who live without hope.*"

Wendell had started with the engine and worked from the ground up. He messed with the old combustion system and gearbox for hours, giving it a partial overhaul, and installed new plugs. Then he moved on to mechanical, replacing some wiring and other dead parts. Recalling from his earlier days as a part-time auto mechanic working his way through college, he reassembled the brake system on the old beater of a Bug, refit the fuel system using items taken from other wrecks that were previously only part of the landscape, and figured the front and rear suspension, though rusty as hell and likely shot, weren't worth tinkering with. He wriggled and reached the tight access points from every angle he could manage, sometimes falling asleep on the dirty asphalt only to awake to noises of the blowing desert breeze or distant squawking birds and commence his work. Minutes became hours, and hours became days. He lost track of time.

The cooling system likely hadn't functioned in years, but he left that mess alone. He also neglected the front and rear bumpers, seats, windscreens as well as windows because . . . priorities. He eventually jacked the old heap off the ground and refit her with used tires that could hold air and weren't merely hashed rubber framing rusty hubcaps inside and out.

At long last, the moment of truth arrives, and Wendell looks down at his cut-up arms, knuckles, and hands, completely cased in black oil, rust, grease, and grime. Having already filled the Volkswagen with hopefully non-spoiled oil, Wendell fetches a gas can to fill up at the pump and bring it to his newfound lady chariot.

"All right, old girl. Don't disappoint." Wendell exhales sharply and fills the gas tank with five gallons. Then another five. And another two or so, topping it off.

Tossing away the gas can, he strolls to the driver's seat and turns the rusted key. The engine turns over weakly, but it doesn't start.

"Spark plugs are working. Engine, sort of."

He exits the vehicle and looks under the hood for the hundredth time, checking the hoses, connections, levels, and overall state of things. If he has to replace any more hard-to-get-to parts, he'll kill himself and be done with it.

He had already changed out the battery, but alas, he'd try a different one. Yanking another one from off the shelf inside the shop, he replaces it again, clamping the red cable to positive and black to negative.

"All right." Wendell huffs and seats himself in the driver's seat.

From all the mouse and rat droppings covering the torn-up upholstery, it's abundantly clear that Wendell hasn't been the only one relying on this lump of old parts. But at this point, he doesn't care about comforts, smells, or aesthetics. He just needs this damn car to start.

Taking a few moments to utter some silent, rudimentary, and incomplete prayer, he turns the key again, shutting his eyes in the hope of ignition.

As the engine heaves, the whirring and whining noises are more prominent, and nightmares of different problems, including a failing alternator, haunt him.

"Just start, you piece of—!"

The engine turns over with a sputter and a kick, and the old girl lives again.

Confounded, Wendell catches his breath and rests his head on the steering wheel. *Has something actually gone my way?*

After a minute, Wendell gets out of the car.

Leaving it running, he wanders inside the station one last time to relieve himself and grab some food, snacks, and drinks for the road.

Approaching the still-abandoned counter, Wendell reaches into his wallet and leaves a small wad of cash for the provisions he's taken. "For whenever you come out of the bathroom again, old man."

Wendell nods, and heads back outside. Only now does he notice it's dusk, just after sunset and twilight.

Hopefully the new headlights I installed are working, is all he can think as he peers out at the gray-blue horizon and that dark desert highway.

He brushes away the mouse pellets and throws his goods on the passenger seat before putting the car in gear. It rolls forward sluggishly. He steps on the gas, and the Bug bumbles forward.

"Please work." He flips on the lights, and they light up brilliantly.

"*We're in business.* Ha Ha Ha! We're in business!"

He rolls to the highway's edge, the gas pumps to his right, and nurses the brake pedal. He looks in both directions, east and west. West is where he came from. West will take him back to the Hotel California. He takes another moment, brooding over the question: *Which way?*

He draws a deep, cleansing breath, filling his lungs, then lets the air out slowly.

"I'm coming back to you, Jeanine. But first, *Vegas.*"

Still no cars in either direction. Not since Lewis.

Wendell turns the steering wheel to the right and presses the gas pedal, easing onto the highway, slow at first, then picking up speed. He heads east down the road.

He has a friend he could stop in on who lives in Vegas. Clarence. It might save him from having to stay at another lodging. Wendell smiles, just thinking of him. Clarence was an old business associate and hang-out buddy, though years ago, he'd gotten out, got himself married, and started a family. Still, he'd probably let Wendell crash on his couch for a night or two while he takes care of some things, makes sure he's clear of any heat, calls a tow service to retrieve his Challenger, and secures a more reliable ride back to his life in California. And who knows? Maybe Ava could come with him or meet him back in LA.

Things are looking up.

"Sin City, here we come." Wendell thinks of the irony and smiles. *Sin City.* Out of the fire, and into the frying pan. He laughs out loud, a stronger tinge of crazy in his voice than he would like to admit. This whole ordeal was messing with his mind and, in fact, his entire demeanor. He hated always being self-aware but knew he was losing it. After driving for several long minutes, Wendell realizes how silent the desert is at night, even with the clunking, rattling, and rumbling of the VW Bug as it rolls over the open asphalt. Some music would be nice, but Wendell looks down and remembers the busted radio. *Of course.* This would be a lengthy and dreary ride alone and without music.

However, this drive proved much more pleasant than that hellish walk through the desert to the gas station without enough water. Thank the Lord; Lewis had shown up, that fat, sweaty angel in the desert. And now

Wendell had plenty of snacks and drinks to keep himself satisfied.

After all, he would get out of this godforsaken desert, and return to his life in LA, un-ideal as it was. The highway stretches for miles ahead, and Wendell begins to hum to himself. Some classic rock tunes. Some alternative.

The old Bug crests one rolling desert hill, only to reveal another and another. The car doesn't go nearly as fast as he'd like over the open highway, but considering its state before Wendell dragged it from the grave, he can't complain.

He thinks about the old man and the gas station and wonders if he's gone fifteen miles yet in the opposite direction. And just as that thought crosses his mind, he notices a small light up ahead in the distance and has a sudden sense of déjà vu.

This particular portion of the landscape seems hauntingly familiar.

Even the tiny light looks familiar—a light he's seen before, though not through as dirty a windshield.

As he approaches, the light becomes several lights, then many. It's a resort.

A hotel.

But not just any hotel.

He continues to drive closer, and his horror is justified.

Spreading out there toward the *eastern* horizon just off the two-lane highway.

"Can't be."

The Hotel California.

Hotel
California

12

Chapter Twelve

A Volkswagen Bug had never torn into a hotel drive as loudly, swiftly, or recklessly as Wendell's newly resurrected wreck, squealing and fishtailing to an abrupt halt just past those pretentious main doors with their polished gold finish.

The Beetle hops the curb in Wendell's rush for answers, but it's difficult for him to care—or even see past the metaphorical smoke and fumes emanating from his every facial orifice. His ears ring, and he shakes like he's just lost a fistfight with his doomed destiny.

The valet approaches him with yet another of those infuriatingly fake smiles. "Mr. Meyers, glad to have you back." He looks at the old beater, his expression dropping to a new level of pretend. "And I see you found a new set of wheels."

Wendell tosses the keys on the ground past his feet as the doorman promptly pushes the main doors ajar. "Ah, Mr. Mey—"

"Don't." Wendell holds up a threatening pointer finger at the young man and hastens into the lobby, marching straight to the front desk.

"Mr. Meyers," says the concierge, "Welcome back."

"Don't give me that. What is this place?!" Wendell fumes. "I want answers."

The two desk clerks glance at one another with a hint of confusion or standoffishness as Wendell's impatience bubbles to its boiling point.

"The . . . Hotel Calif—" the tall one starts.

"No, uh-uh," Wendell brings back that threatening finger and leans in acrimoniously. *"What . . . is . . . this . . . place?"*

"I'm sorry, Mr. Meyers, if you could be more specific. If you are dissatisfied with your stay or if there is anything we—"

"Anyth—" Wendell drops his head, huffing. "Anything you can do? Uh, yeah. You can fix my damn car and get me the hell outta here!"

The concierge clears his throat. "I'm afraid we do not have a mechanic on staff, Mr. Meyers, but if we—"

"'Course you don't. But there's Gus, right? Just up the road? What, fifteen miles as the crow flies? Why don't you give him a ring? Call him down to service half the derelict cars sitting in your garage. He only left that shop years ago—according to the ghost of an old man. By the way, tell him to come down to pick up his Volkswagen. I got it running! Better yet, why don't I take *your* car? Or *yours?!*" He points to the other receptionist, who takes a defensive step back. "Or do you all live here like a bunch o' trust fund crazies?"

"Mr. Meyers, you can check out anytime—"

"Really? Where's your manager?"

"W-would you like to speak with the day manager? The night man?"

"You know what? I would. Could you please fetch him? I've got a few concerns I'd like to discuss. Some complaints I'd like to file."

"Very well, Mr. Meyers. We'll call him right down. In the meantime, I can offer you a complimentary spa certificate. Perhaps a massage—"

"A . . . are you kidding me?" Wendell bursts out in a strained chuckle. "A massage?"

"You seem dissatisfied with your stay thus far. We only want to make you comfortable."

"Comfortable?" Oozing frustration and sarcasm, Wendell nods, unwilling to wait. "Yeah, great." Then he storms off toward the elevator and staircase.

"Uh, M-Mr. Meyers?! Mr. Meyers? Would you still like to speak with the manager?"

"Damn right I would," he mutters under his breath. "If I don't find a way to leave first." Wendell punches the button for the elevator and waits for the doors to open, then stomps inside. For the first time since his arrival from the station, he realizes what he probably looks like and definitely smells like.

Shit.

"They'll all think I'm crazy," he utters. Yet, if he's honest with himself, he doesn't much care after the hell he's been through.

The time has come to take Ava up on her offer for a ride . . . perhaps after a quick shower. That is, if her car even starts.

* * *

"Bring your alibis," was the last thing Lamb had said to Gamble before he lawyered up and locked himself inside an FBI interrogation room with three non-descript men representing his obscenely expensive counsel. The room, equipped with no cameras, microphones, and no panes of one-way glass, would give them nothing useful.

"From here on out, he's not going to say a damn thing," Lamb tells Solarin, who nods his agreement. "At least, to us. If only we had a letter from the CEO to a record label with Gamble's name on it offering a bribe in exchange for airplay," she said, half sarcastically. "We need to get this to the DA right away. With this evidence, they'll be able to build a strong case against SkyBox and all its officers. Come on, Solarin. Let's bring these corrupt bastards to justice."

Despite its brevity, Solarin chuckles, appreciating Lamb's sudden sense of humor. But then their faces sink to match the depressing dim lighting of the government facility around them, accepting the stark reality before them.

"We're never going to find enough evidence to convict," Lamb says, drawing a long breath. "Are we?"

Solarin stands next to her with his arms folded reverently and sighs. "Nope. They'll stall. Drag it on. Point fingers. Try to hang it on the peons, affiliates, accounting errors, and coincidences. No, I've seen it a hundred times. Companies like this? With these kinds of connections? As God is my witness, corrupt businessmen like Gamble get what's coming to them, but in a place like the City of Angels, it does not come in this lifetime. Not *usually.*"

Lamb only mildly appreciates Solarin's religious sense of eventual justice. "Guess that leaves us with only two more boxes to check before we shut this down and move on." They say the names together and in unison: "Jeremey Bianchi and Wendell Meyers."

Lamb scratches the side of her lip, assuming a deep dive into these men's possessions, relationships, and whereabouts would also end in disappointment. "A cash manager and a chief accounting officer."

Solarin corrects her: "*Former . . .* chief accounting officer."

"Right." Lamb takes a step toward the hallway leading to the main office, and Solarin follows.

"Which one do you want to start with?" Lamb asks.

Solarin thinks for only a moment. "Meyers. Let's start with Meyers."

* * *

Ava wasn't in her room, so Wendell traipses out to the pool deck amidst another happening party where everyone is living it up to the fullest, throwing all inhibitions to a warm, subtle wind and dancing to a throbbing mix of droning beats. This time, it's more crowded than before, which is surprising considering how many people attended the first party Wendell had been to. And he hadn't seen any new arrivals in the drive or lobby since.

Wendell doesn't search frantically, but he does feel a bit frantic as he cases the loud, excited, and scantily clad partygoers searching for a charming lady who had claimed to own a working ride. And a *Mercedes-Benz* at that. This time, she would drive and break the curse of Wendell's own making. She would get him out of here—*for good*.

Brandy Alexanders. Harvey Wallbangers. Piña Coladas. Pink Squirrels. Tequila Sunrises. All happily poured. All verily enjoyed. And no complaints from across the elated mob of glistening bodies. Everyone's overly indulgent self-gratification, social mixing, and fun renders Wendell's search most difficult. He weaves on and off the winding sidewalks, through the grass, over concrete partitions, and around sprawling cabanas intermingled with posts and hanging towels.

These people are cultist crazy, Wendell tells himself. But here he is, among them.

Stepping over the corners of lawn chairs with cooking sunbathers, Wendell receives invitation after invitation from women plenty easy on the eyes. On any other occasion, he would likely fall to their whims, give in to their requests for company, and so much more.

But he is here for Ava and *only* Ava.

After what feels like half a day of searching, Wendell nearly gives up and sits poolside, cooling off his feet in the azure water. A waiter takes his order and, soon after, delivers a Pink Lady. Wendell removes the little umbrella and sips it slowly. He continues to look around casually for the girl of his dreams. Perhaps she's avoiding him. Maybe she doesn't want to be found. He could easily see her moving on to enjoy the company of the next successful man to come along and catch her eye, never mind how painful it is to admit it to himself. She's likely that kind of a girl. *Too good to be true.* But these thoughts aren't new to Wendell.

"There's my man! What a nice surprise!" Ava shrieks and runs over from behind him, carefully balancing her margarita wine cocktail in one hand.

Wendell whirls around and jumps to his feet, spilling his drink all over his arm. "Oh, come on."

"Wendell, you devil! Where have you been?"

Sure enough, she is with two other men. *Beautiful, young* men, though they seem friendly towards him.

Even still, she pushes up against Wendell and rubs her slender fingers through his sweaty hair, their noses almost touching. "And your hair's all wet—have you been swimming without me?"

"Took a shower."

"You're very sunburned," she says, playfully judgmental. "Remind me to rub some sunscreen on you. And you can do me."

Wendell glances at the other two guys awkwardly standing there, but they smile back unassumingly.

"Sure. Ava, do you mind if we talk?"

"Yeah babe, what do you want to talk about? Did you get your car fixed?"

"That's what I want to discuss."

"Oh?" She gives him a devilish smirk. "You still wanna go for that long drive?"

Wendell looks around, inhales, and exhales, then faces her squarely, grabbing her by the arms.

She looks down at his firm hands uncomfortably. "What's the matter?" *What are you doing?*

"Can we get out of here?"

"What do you mean? We're in the middle of a party . . . unless you're saying what I think you're saying?"

"I just want to spend some time with you . . ." Again, he looks at the young men waiting behind her. Their gaze has already fallen on a group of girls playing in the pool. ". . . *Alone.*"

"Oh," she says, half blushing. "Well. Better not call the captain to bring me more wine. Or will *you* be driving?"

"Sorry boys," Ava says to her handsome chaperons, slurring her words only slightly. "I've got a date with this one."

Wendell knows she's drunk, but will take advantage of the situation, nonetheless. "Have I told you how pretty you are?" He asks.

She wraps a lean arm around his shoulders, and they saunter easily back toward the hotel. "Tell me again."

"Ava, you are so beautiful; you make swans want to kill themselves."

She giggles like a schoolgirl.

"You're so fit; you make gazelles want to break their own legs."

She nearly snorts but catches herself.

A few passersby glance over and grin at them as they pass.

Wendell thinks up his next complement watching all the people around, young and old, but mostly old. "If we were playing *Clue*, and everyone here was dead, I'd guess it was . . . *Ava*, on the *pool deck*, with the *pink and orange bikini on her smoking hot body*."

They laugh together and continue into the building, where they make a stop in Ava's room to grab her car keys, mess around a little, and eventually head toward the parking garage to her awaiting silver steed.

Arms up catching the wind, Ava shouts out in delight as they soar over the highway. *West* this time. She is snuggled into the passenger seat of her own Mercedes, still dressed for the pool, hammered, and ready for a bash.

Wendell doesn't tell her this will be an extended road trip back to LA. He doesn't tell her he's not returning to the Hotel California. He hadn't had her pack any bags because he could buy her some food and clothes on the road. That bit could have been better thought out, and she'd hate him for it, but he had to get out of there. And he didn't want to go without her.

He cranks the tunes on the radio, and more than breaks the speed limit. Ava hoots and hollers and dances drunkenly in her seat. The whole ordeal rather turns Wendell on, but his main focus is the road. The open road. Miles of desert ahead. Sand. Dirt. *Nothing.*

"Where are we going?" Ava finally asks.

Wendell doesn't answer her for a while, so she asks again.

Wendell looks at her, and smiles. "Anywhere," he says. "Nowhere."

She closes her eyes and stretches her lithe neck, her hair fluttering back like the wings of a bird.

This could be Heaven, Wendell thinks to himself as he watches her, but then something catches his eye up ahead.

What the hell?!"

Someone standing in the middle of the road! *Jeanine?!* Wendell swerves hard left, then right to avoid hitting her, over-correcting, and the Mercedes skids across the highway, flying off the pavement into sagebrush, bucking, throwing them around inside the cabin, and fishtailing to an eventual slamming halt into a rock.

When the dust settles and nothing can be heard but a calm desert breeze, Wendell stirs.

He's bloody. Bruised. Aching. But conscious. He finds Ava in a similar state, but she's out cold.

"Ava? *Ava?!* He scrambles over to her and checks her pulse, but there isn't one. *"AVA! NO! Wake up! Wake up! Do you hear me?!"*

He crumples over in a heap on top of her, his bloody forehead resting on her naked shoulder.

She's gone. Her body is still. Lifeless. *Dead.*

Wendell sobs, loud at first, and then quietly and to himself once he's out of energy.

After some time passes—if there were such a thing in this godforsaken desert—he opens his eyes again, slowly. The sun is blinding. However, in the distance, there is some movement.

A person walking along the side of the road.

"Jeanine?"

With much pain and effort, Wendell crawls out of the car and stands beside it.

She's walking toward him along the roadside but is still far away, so Wendell tries to close the gap, hobbling along past scrub oak and other thick, scratchy desert plant life. He's not quite sure about the seriousness of his injuries, but he can walk, so he does.

As he approaches what looks to be his long-time friend, he notices something *off* about her; she walks like she's not all there, like a zombie of sorts.

Wendell remembers the dream in the saloon with all the dead bodies and wonders what it might have meant if anything.

"Jeanine?" He tries to call out to her, but his voice fails. He swallows hard and tries again. "Jeanine!"

She doesn't look at him, only keeps ambling along.

Wendell picks up his pace and approaches her on the highway before she can pass him. It *is* Jeanine, but she's not herself.

"Jeanine," he says. "Jeanine, I've had an accident. Can you hear me? *I said I've been in an accident."*

She presses forward, but now she's in the shoulder.

Wendell thinks back to just before the crash. "Jeanine, why were you on the road? Jeanine, you were in the middle of the road! What were you—What are doing here?! Jeanine?"

He grabs her shoulder and forces her to stop and look at him, her head bobbling slightly. "It's Wendell. Why—?"

Her deadpan gaze looks off to her left, then through Wendell, then at someone walking up behind him.

Wendell turns around to see who it is.

A large, hardened-looking man that could easily pass as a truck driver or oil rig worker with blood running up and down the front of his jaw, shirt, and dirty trousers steps up to him.

"Who are you?"

The man sneers and belts Wendell in the face, knocking him out with overwhelming force.

All goes black, and Wendell falls by the roadside.

* * *

Wendell awakes in bed, in his room in the Hotel California. He aches, but not like before. He comes to slowly, methodically, groping at his forehead, his legs, remembering the injuries, the limp, the crash. He rolls up into a seated position at the side of the bed, planting his feet on the hard-pressed carpet. His toes feel fine, as do his feet. He puts some pressure on his legs and stands up straight and tall. He further explores his body, finding no blood, cuts, or gashes. And then he remembers *her*. Stiff and numb in the passenger's seat of her own Mercedes.

"Ava."

His doing. Or was it even real? He wishes to God that it wasn't and, simultaneously, questions what reality is. Who can he trust if not himself? What can he trust?

Wendell drops his head momentarily, replaying the horrible scene in his racing mind, praying it was merely a nightmare. He would have to verify.

He wears pajamas but doesn't remember ever putting them on.

He strips and hurries to the closet to get dressed, then rushes out of the room and down the hall to the elevators.

The hallways spin as he staggers along, like the gently moving tunnels in carnival fun houses that throw off one's equilibrium.

He knocks hard on the door to Ava's room, his breathing and blinking frenetic.

"Please," he whispers, resting his whole body against the door frame. "Please, Ava. Please answer the door."

He nearly breaks down to the point of tears before he hears her sing-song voice approaching. "Just a moment."

A jolt of adrenaline eases him back and away from the door. He stands upright, wiping at his eyes, straightening his hair, swallowing the despair that drowned him only a moment ago.

The door swings ajar, and there she stands.

A vision.

A beauty.

An angel in a silken nightgown framed with flowing locks. Even without a spec of makeup, her natural beauty floors him. "Hey there, Wendell. You alright?"

"Uh," he swallows again, and clears his throat. "Uh, yes. Hello, Ava."

"Fine morning," she says with a smile. "How'd you sleep?"

"Uh . . ." He still can't believe it. *Her. Here. Alive.* "Fine. A—fine. I slept . . . Hey, you wanna—?"

"Come in, Wendell. You look like you need some company."

Peering into her patient auburn eyes, Wendell finally relaxes and relents. "I do."

"You want some juice? Coffee?"

He enters, and Ava shuts the door behind them.

Hours later, Wendell wanders into the hotel lobby and approaches the reception area, the front desk still manned by the same two clerks.

When they see Wendell, they lean back, expecting the worst from him. But instead, he rests a hand on the polished red mahogany and asks, "Is that complimentary massage certificate still available?"

The concierge glances at the other, then back at Wendell, and smiles with relief. "Um, why yes, Mr. Meyers, let me fetch that for you. Feeling better, I presume?"

Wendell, with dead eyes, looks up at the man. "Right as rain."

13

Chapter Thirteen

"Nice studio apartment for downtown," Lamb says. "Especially for someone living alone. He must do well for himself."

"Heh," Solarin nods, "Yep. Sure beats my rambler in Westlake. Wonder if he'd like to make a trade. Maybe my kids could have their own bedrooms."

"Mailbox is overflowing," Lamb says. "He hasn't been home for a while."

"Maybe he's on the *'Lamb,'*" Solarin says, intentionally making a bad joke.

"Not if it's *me* we're talking about."

Having obtained a search warrant from the local judge based on Gamble's testimony, the two men's positions at the company, the dead bodies, and the ledgers from Phillips' storage unit, the probable cause was enough to be convincing. Still, they felt lucky to have the written affidavits nonetheless because there were no guarantees they would find anything pointing to the fact that Wendell Meyers or Jeremey Bianchi committed any crime. The legalese detailing what they were allowed to search for and where had also been left fairly wide open as to each residential address, making their jobs easier.

Solarin and Lamb step through the wide entryway into the kitchen and dining area of Wendell Meyer's flat, rubber gloves in place and plastic evidence bags ready. They carefully and methodically case through the apartment, room by room, closet by closet, draw by drawer.

Lamb notes the avocado-green floor, surprisingly working against the avant-garde-styled interior. The earth tones and multi-color accents with low-slung furniture give a glimpse into his unique personality. Amusing, perhaps even a little spicy—if accountants could ever be considered spicy—but still sophisticated.

Despite all that, the quiet stillness of the apartment unsettles Officer Lamb while Solarin works calmly and collectedly across from her.

In the search for Mr. Meyers and building out his profile, Lamb had contacted the parents hours before. They still lived in Florida, where Meyers grew up. Lamb had also called siblings and known acquaintances from his distant and recent past, which bore little fruit. The mom and dad, stalwart self-proclaimed Christians, apparently had little contact with their son over recent years. They had said they couldn't convince him to visit for holidays or birthdays, though they knew he could afford it. In tying up the conversation, Wendell's mother had said, "We never much approved of his choices since he graduated High School." And his father added, "He's the prodigal son that never bothered to return."

Lamb and Solarin find some bottles stashed in the kitchen cabinets, more than one might use for cooking, but not necessarily enough to label the man an alcoholic. No hard drugs or fetishes are readily apparent. No blatantly damning evidence to speak of. For all intents and purposes, Wendell Meyers, though arguably wayward, proved to be rather average at first glimpse.

They make it into Wendell's home office space, weave around the large sepia-colored desk, open and begin flipping through his file cabinets, pulling out old business ledgers, bank account statements, and tax documents. Everything seems in order at first glance; this man was organized and had everything collated, labeled, and alphabetized by section and topic. A man of finance and certainly a professional. But also a loner. Lamb assumes that hunch is more of a feeling than any of the paperwork might suggest.

As Lamb thinks it, Solarin states, "This Meyers fellow is the most organized accountant I've come across. Maybe even to the point of obsessive."

Lamb nods and turns back to her stacks of hanging folders and files, quickly realizing the need to fetch more boxes for processing back at the office.

As she fossicks deeper, she finds more of Meyer's personal items, such as his birth certificate, passport, and Social Security card. She holds them all up for Solarin to see.

"It doesn't look like he was planning on going anywhere. And if he did, he didn't take much with him. I've even got some of his blank checkbooks here. Nothing's locked up. It's strange."

"It is odd," Lamb says. "If he was so mixed up in the SkyBox payola scandal, or worst case, the mob, why would he just leave everything here for us to find? Why wouldn't he burn it, or at least shred it? Erase any indication of his involvement? Do you think he planned—*or plans*—on turning himself in?"

Solarin looks up a moment, considering. "Don't know." The senior officer moves off into the next room as Lamb continues to box and tag the last few drawers of documentation.

After twenty minutes, Solarin's voice rings out from another room with a slight far-off echo.

Lamb drops what she's doing, puts a hand over her sidearm, and moves into the living room and lounge area to follow his voice. "Solarin?"

"I'm out in the garage! Come take a look at this. Tell me what you think."

She finds the interior access door to the garage through the pantry and laundry room and finds Solarin standing next to what appears to be some type of muscle car hiding under a canvas covering. Lamb walks down the steps of Meyer's tidy garage/shop and circles the vehicle. "This wasn't his only ride," she says.

"Nope," Solarin reaches down and grabs the canvas with both hands, "But I bet it was his favorite." He yanks off the cover to reveal a black Dodge Challenger with two broad racing stripes running down the center. It's in pristine condition, as though it's never been driven. It looks like it's only been taken out a handful of times—cherry red interior, genuine leather, dusty dashboard.

"New tires, fancy wheels. Think it runs?" Lamb asks.

"Oh, I guarantee it runs. Likely purrs. The money this guy has?"

"Has?" Lamb asks, "Or *had?*"

Solarin purses his lips and peers back at her, his hands still holding up the dust-covered canvas.

In unison, their eyes fall back on the beauty of a muscle car, which has been completely abandoned.

* * *

Wendell's mind had climbed quickly and dangerously to the top of a precarious precipice. And for some reason—either having worked on the VW Bug for hours on end, absorbing an unusual amount of the sun's UV rays at the resort, or feeling the effects of his violent dream of the car crash with Ava—his body hurts.

He wanders down a hotel corridor he hasn't been to, searching for the in-house spa among the lower levels. He has an appointment and he doesn't want to miss it. The surroundings are new but with that same patterned carpet and wallpaper all around that he can't quite seem to escape.

He begins to whisper to himself, *"Plenty of room. Plenty of space. Never mind the doom. It's such a lovely place. Plenty of room. Plenty of space. Never mind the doom. It's such a lovely place. Never mind the—"*

Up ahead, at the end of a long hallway, he finally sees the wood-painted French doors with "*Body & Soul Spa*" inscribed in white, centered on the frosted glass in a fancy script font face. "Ah, here we are."

As someone who physically internalizes his emotions to some degree—sans his outburst at reception and other occasional exceptions—and desperate to find relief, he wonders why he hasn't sought out masseuses before, back in LA. *Or was it massage therapists?* He can never remember the socially acceptable conventions.

He'd tried a few things to remedy the big muscle knots in his back, such as yoga and meditation, even occasionally going to the gym, but they weren't for him. Aspirin and Tylenol, however, had become regular residents in his medicine cabinet. Not to mention the booze. Anything to take the edge off.

But now he would enjoy the ultimate act of self-care. And it was 'on the house' to boot. So what better time to try out a massage? If he liked it, he might ask for massage gift certificates instead of material objects for the holidays. Not that his painfully limited pool of friends ever really asked.

Wendell reaches for the door.

"Welcome to the Body & Soul Spa," says a pleasant young woman, practically before he steps inside.

"Thank you." Wendell glances around and slowly approaches the front desk. The space boasts a minimalistic, modern design aesthetic with a flare of California retro and tastefully subtle surfboard motifs. Occasional wafts of peppermint, lavender, and eucalyptus reach his nostrils.

"What can I do for you?" she asks with a brilliant smile.

"I believe I have an appointment . . . for a massage," Wendell says.

"Let me have a look." She refers to her files.

Wendell lightly taps a finger on the white desk and continues to look around for others, but there's only the receptionist.

"Yes, here we are. It looks like they called it down yesterday. Wendell?" She hands him a clipboard.

"Yes."

"Go ahead and fill that out, and your massage therapist will be with you shortly. Are you okay with a female therapist?"

Wendell takes the clipboard and looks up at the young woman. "Uh, that would be preferred, actually."

"Great."

He takes the pen and begins to fill in his information but stops at a question as to what type of massage he's looking for.

"What *type* of massage?" he asks out loud. "Isn't a massage a massage?"

"Oh, there are dozens of different types," says the girl. "Thai, sports, reflexology, deep tissue, shiatsu. All designed to aid your body in different ways. Swedish is most common."

"All right. Let's do that."

The girl nods with a grin.

He finishes and hands the clipboard back.

"Thanks, Wendell. Go ahead and have a seat, and she'll be right out."

Wendell sits on a soft white loveseat in the far corner of the open room. He looks at a little fountain next to him on a table with tiny exotic desert cactus growing out between black polished stones. The slight sound of trickling water is all there is.

Flashes of the Mercedes fishtailing and flying off the road play in his mind. Ava's lifeless body, covered in blood, cuts, and bruises, slumped against the broken passenger window. Wendell lowers his head and breathes deep, attempting to push away the memory. Make-believe or not, it affected him.

Leaning back, he wonders why he's the only one here. It seems like a nice place.

The girl at the desk watches him periodically from the corner of her eye as she works. What she could be working on, Wendell has no idea.

Finally, he hears a door open from around the curving hallway to the right of the welcome foyer and the crisp footsteps of sharp shoes on tile. A brown-haired woman approaches that, from a purely physical standpoint, might give Ava a run for her money. "Wendell?" she says, glancing down at him, then taking the clipboard from the girl at the desk.

"Yeah, that's me." He stands and pops his neck.

"Hi, I'm Kendra." She reaches out a well-manicured hand for Wendell to walk up and take. "I'll be your massage therapist today."

He can't help but notice how warm and smooth her skin feels. "Great. Nice to meet you."

"Right this way." There is something mysterious in her tone, her expression. Something concealing, yet profoundly inviting.

She walks ahead of him as they pass several other unlabeled frosted glass doors to their right. Wendell assumes they are other rooms hiding massage tables, saunas, or mani/pedi stations.

"This is us." The last room on the left. Kendra stops and spins on her heel, gesturing for him to enter.

The room is dimly lit and well-designed. Soft, classical music plays over the speakers in the ceiling. This room also has a tiny fountain, a sink, bottles of lotions and oils, and a warming oven with a stack of black towels next to it. In the room's center is the massage table with a folded white towel sitting on top.

Kendra glances down at the clipboard. "Swedish. Full body. What else can I do for you today?"

Wendell gulps. "Uh, heh, what do you mean?"

"Would you like any add-ons?"

Wendell had heard of massage parlors offering 'above and beyond' services for special tips, but he thought those types of places existed primarily outside the country. He shakes his head, embarrassed at his naivety. If such things happened here, he wanted her to say it. "Such as . . . ?"

Kendra lets out a giggle, those perfectly symmetrical eyes difficult to read. "Oils? Hot towels?"

"Oh, right, uh, whatever you think. I don't know, give me the works. I'm pretty sore." He rubs his shoulder and neck.

"Sure. Do you prefer it deep or relaxing?"

"Split the difference."

"Any areas you'd like me to target?"

"Wherever you can find some knots, I suppose."

She smiles. "Fair enough. Strip to your comfort level. You can put your clothes in that bin and you may use the towel to cover yourself. We'll start face down. And I'll be right back."

"Thanks."

She exits, and Wendell follows her instructions, undressing to his birthday suit, lying face down on the table, and using the towel to cover his bottom half. He wonders if he should have used the restroom before, but it's too late now.

A few minutes later, she lightly knocks on the door.

"Come in."

He rests his head in the face cradle, peering down at the carpet, before closing his eyes and focusing on slowing his breathing. *I do need some relaxation,* he tells himself. Crashing the Mercedes, losing Ava, the trauma, it all felt so real. And it still hadn't registered or processed completely.

She walks around the table, squeezes out some lotion or oil, rubs her hands together, and presses down on his shoulders and back.

Her firm touch is intoxicating, and as she works, Wendell discovers that her forearms are even smoother than her hands.

"How is that pressure?" she asks, expertly gliding over the skin of his back.

"Heavenly," Wendell says. "Thank you."

"Just let me know if I'm pushing too hard."

He tries to nod, but the face cradle makes it awkward.

She gets into the tight knots and sore muscles around his neck, shoulder blades, and lower spine, so he tries even harder to relax despite the welcome pain.

He lets the music and the consistent sense of touch soothe him, almost to sleep. Almost, because, on top of the crash, he can't shake the question of how he drove both east and west on that highway for miles yet still ended up here. He always subscribed to the philosophy that there's no problem you can't hide or run away from, so these unanswered questions and feelings of being trapped drive him crazy.

She eventually moves down to focus on his glutes, which he enjoys immensely, then his arms and the backs of his legs.

When it comes time to turn over, the massage therapist lifts the towel covering him and holds it up to block her view of Wendell. *Very professional.* He groggily flips around, thoroughly enjoying himself but hoping that won't show in his lower regions. She places the towel back on top of him and commences to work on the front portions of his legs, one at a time.

Wendell settles back in and tries to relax, though his upper thighs and feet seem a bit ticklish. Her slow and sensual technique helps with that to the point he can take it without squirming around or saying anything.

When she gets to his second leg, her soft hands seem to roughen up a bit, and he wonders if she might need more lotion. As the friction between her skin and his intensifies, he's tempted to look down or suggest she use more product to oil him up, but he's not quite sure if it's appropriate or conventional to open his eyes mid-massage. He doesn't, after all, feel comfortable questioning her professionalism, approach, or technique, as it's been so wonderful up to this point. And her being attractive makes him wonder if she might think him a pervert if he watches her while she works on him, even if only for a few seconds.

The resistance, however, intensifies, and not just from her hands but her arms and elbows as well, to the point of chafing. Even scraping.

"Just relax," she says, gently shaking his thigh with her coarse grasp.

He barely opens his eyes.

He can only see the dark silhouette of her hair and shoulders through his spying slits, and the dim lighting makes it difficult to make her out completely, but the pain from her rubbing sticks of fingers becomes unbearable, so he opens his full gaze.

Expecting to see the beautiful Kendra as he sits up, a rotted female corpse with ratty brown hair and missing eyes has taken her place and gapes back at him through decayed flesh, nasty teeth, and cracked fingernails.

"The hell?!" He grasps behind him and backs away from the creature, kicking his legs out of her skeletal clutches, and falls backward off the table. She's blocking the exit, so he grabs the towel off the floor and plows past her, pushing the living corpse against the wall and throwing open the door.

He slides and crashes into the hallway against the opposing wall, naked and frantic.

"Wendell!" she cries, but her voice is like a colony of screeching bats. "What's wrong? What did I do?"

Wendell sprints down the arching hallway past all the other frosted doors but slips and stumbles along the way. Turning back, he sees Kendra coming out after him, but she's no longer a walking, talking corpse. She looks normal again. Even beautiful. But he's not about to stick around and ask questions.

"Your clothes!" Kendra shouts. "You forgot your clothes!"

Wendell sails past the girl at the desk and makes for the exit.

"Wendell?" The young woman stands as he streaks out of the place.

He doesn't have a plan, so he runs through the hallways and hotel corridors and up to his room, paying no mind to staff or other hotel guests he passes, half naked with only a white towel to cover his loins and backside.

Room service could fetch his clothes later.

He wouldn't be making any more visits to the Body & Soul Spa. More than anything, he needs an explanation. Yet he knows he won't get a suitable one from anybody here. Or perhaps a psychological evaluation would shed further light on this hellish circumstance he's found himself in. That's the more terrifying nag.

Is it truly this place? Wendell stresses, slamming his hand over the

B.C. NAILES

doorknob to his room. *Or is it me?!*

Just now, he realizes he left his room key in his pants pocket, tucked neatly in the bin across from the massage table.

"Oh, crap."

He looks down and lifts the towel, bending over to examine the front portions of his legs. They are red, irritated, and covered in subtle scratch marks, the right leg much worse than the left.

"It was real," he utters under his breath. "It's not just me."

Or is it both? He looks up at the door, upset over the whole experience. He notices a cleaning maid's cart way down the hall, almost on the other side of the building, opposite the centrally located elevator bank. Shaking his head, he re-secures the towel around his waist and makes for the cart, hoping the maid will have a master key and praying she won't spontaneously morph into a killer zombie as she lets him back into his room.

"Excuse me, ma'am?!"

14

Chapter Fourteen

Wendell sits alone at the ballroom bar, in the very same spot where the lovely brunette had come on to him days or weeks previous—he has no idea. That is if it even transpired the way he remembers it. He stares down into his nearly empty glass, gently swirling the ice cubes around. He takes a breath of self-pity and lets it out like someone who lost their thirty-third round at the slots.

Leo wanders from behind him, recognizes him, and takes a seat on the barstool beside his. "Wendell, my boy, haven't seen you around for a bit."

Wendell nods. "I've been here and there. Not far."

Leo chuckles. "Yeah, not far." He motions to the bartender. "I'll have what he's havin'."

The bartender drops his cleaning rag and gets after it.

"You don't want what I'm having," Wendell says. "Trust me."

"Whatever the man who streaks out of a massage parlor and runs up and down the place in naught but a hand towel . . . Yeah, I'll have what he's havin'."

"You heard about that."

"My boy, everyone's heard about that."

Wendell grins, a little embarrassed but not enough to care.

"Oh, come on, man, you gotta drop the 'wo is me' act. It's been long enough. I mean, look at this place. What more could you want? What more is there? A nine-to-five? Dirty diapers? Backstabbers and door-to-door salesmen? Politics?"

"Politics?"

"Yeah, you haven't even heard mention of elephants or asses since you've been here, am I right?"

Wendell chuckles. "I suppose not."

"Damn right I'm right. Republicans . . . Democrats? *Who needs it?* Just *talkin'* about politics feels like a waste of time. So I'll ask again—what more could you want?"

Wendell sighs. "Reality . . . truth." He finally looks over at Leo. *"Happiness."*

Leo takes his drink from the barkeep. "What's truer than the touch of a woman? A cool swim on a hot afternoon? The open road, the wind in your hair?" He lifts his glass in a mock 'cheers.' "The buzz of the perfectly mixed drink?"

"Oh, I dunno, fulfillment? Family? *Freedom?*"

"You're not even close to your family. And you're a single guy!"

"How do you know that?"

"Because you told me. Don't you remember? And just look at you. Family man? I think not."

Had he told him? Or anyone? Wendell puts a hand on his forehead, unable to recall. The topic of his strained child/parent relationship doesn't seem like one he'd bring up in casual conversation with someone he'd just met. But then he supposes he's known Leo for a quite some time. Or has he? The matter grows foggy.

"Besides," says Leo, "They're illusions. Taradiddle. Nobody's free. Not really. Not here. Not out there. How long have I been waiting for my family to show up? I'll tell you." He bursts out angrily, "An eternity!"

The bartender, back to wiping down rinsed-off glasses glances at them.

Leo gathers himself, hunching his shoulders. "No, believe you me, it's all a carnival ride. An act. You gotta pay to get on, can't wait to get off, and you're sick while in the seat. All you can hope for are those fleeting little moments of real . . . *nirvana.* But you can't expect them to stick around. Oh no. They're too quick to grab onto. Too slippery to hold."

"No, I think you're wrong," Wendell says bluntly. "Earthly pleasures,

hope without work—Dreams aren't enough."

"What's wrong with dreams?"

He gives the old man a look. "You haven't been in mine lately."

After a moment, Leo leans back and gives him a deadpan stare. "So you're tellin' me you prefer pain over pleasure?"

"Reality is both."

Then, leaning forward, he whispers, "You know what you need?"

Wendell finishes the last sip of his drink and sets down the glass. "No, Leo. Tell me. What do I need?"

The old man reaches into his pocket and pulls out a folded red handkerchief. He sets it on the bar in front of Wendell.

Sighing, Wendell looks down at it. "What's inside the handkerchief, Leo?" *Magic mushrooms? Ecstacy?*

He smiles. "*Escape,* my friend. *Release.* That's what you want, isn't it?" He nods at the offering. "Well, there it is. I'll wager you can find God inside that handkerchief."

It's not the first time someone's offered Wendell a particular product to 'clear his head' or find 'Heaven.'

The bartender looks the other way.

"Thanks, Leo, but I don't want to be the punchline of another cautionary tale. Isn't this place enough?" Wendell puts his hand on the cloth and slides the handkerchief-wrapped drug fix back to the old man.

"You sure?"

"Quite."

"We'll see." Leo takes the handkerchief and stuffs it back in his pocket. "Maybe later, huh? Then who will be the elephant, and who will be the ass?"

"No hard feelings," Wendell says. "I just—"

"My boy, when you reach my age, *hard* feelings don't come even if you want them to."

Both men chuckle awkwardly and have another drink. Surprised, Wendell realizes that he is actually tempted by the old man's offer, and he pauses to reconsider it, not even clear about what it was.

* * *

The nasty sweet smell of garbage wafts by, assaulting the nostrils of both Lamb and Solarin as they pass an alleyway on foot just a few blocks from the firm. Another block over, a homeless man hunches next to a handwritten cardboard sign propped against the concrete and brick. It reads: "*Have you ever felt invisible before?*" The man through his ratty grayish brown mane, eyebrows, and beard sees them and stands to—Lamb assumes—ask for money.

Lamb lowers her forearm from covering her nose and pulls out her clutch to offer the man a five. Solarin patiently stops with her to watch the exchange.

The man's baby blue eyes light up as he sheepishly steps forward, head bowed, to kindly accept the offering. "Oh, th-thank you, ma'am. Very kind of you. I'm not usually here, you know, my f-friends and me. You know, dangerous streets, these."

"Sure," Lamb says.

The man quickly pockets the cash and glances around to make sure none of his fellow vagrants take notice.

Lamb and Solarin continue walking.

"That's sweet of you," Solarin says. "I have trust issues when it comes to those on the streets, or perpetuating panhandling, but I suppose they do tell you in church to err on the side of charity."

"I don't do it for the sake of charity. Did you hear what he said?" Lamb stops a moment to think.

"Yes." Solarin puzzles. "*Dangerous streets.* That's a pretty generic comment about—"

Lamb returns to the homeless man, Solarin right behind her. "Excuse me, sir?"

The man looks up at them defensively as though he knows he's done something wrong.

Lamb softens her expression. "Do you mind if I ask you a few questions?"

The man glances away, his gaze resting on the derelicts eyeing him from across the alley. His bent demeanor suggests he wasn't expecting to have to *earn* her handout. "Be quick about it. Are you f-feds? Cops?"

"Don't worry about that. You're not in any trouble. I just wanted to ask you what you meant when you said these streets are dangerous."

The homeless man scoffs. "Well look around, lady. This ain't exactly Disneyland."

Lamb sighs. "Right. What I mean to say is, have you seen anything recently, over the last few weeks. Any . . . *violence*? Specific incidents? Maybe something that made you feel like you might be in danger? Or someone else?"

The man stares straight ahead, as though he knows something, but doesn't want to say it.

"Please," Lamb says. "Anything. Anything you might remember."

After several moments, Solarin sighs and looks away. "You're wasting your time," he says softly.

Lamb stares at the downtrodden man, but all she sees is fear.

"What's your name?" she asks.

The man looks at her through the corner of his eye. "Earl."

She offers him a hand, knowing full well how dirty his are. "It's nice to meet you, Earl."

The man reluctantly takes it, and they shake with a loose grip.

"You take care of yourself," Lamb says. "Maybe we can talk tomorrow."

Lamb stands erect, and she and Solarin continue down the sidewalk together.

After a minute or so, Solarin gives her a sidelong glance. "What are you thinking about?"

"You ever heard of pareidolia?"

"Pareidolia?" Solarin smiles. "You mean when people claim to see images of saints in toast or found rocks?"

"Or recognize significant images or faces in random patterns."

"Whose face? What are you talking about?"

"I've seen that man before, Officer Solarin. In a photo, on the street, during one of our interviews. Somewhere."

"The homeless guy back there?" Solarin shakes his head. "I haven't seen him. You ask me, we've been looking at too much paperwork, mugshots, spreadsheets in particular. I think sometimes we tend to see patterns where there are none. Primarily in our line of work."

"I think he might know something," Lamb says. "I think he's seen something."

Solarin smiles. "Hunch? Or coply intuition?"

"I'm not a cop," Lamb says.

"Hunch then. We do get them from time to time. Hungry?"

"Starving."

Solarin nods. "What restaurant? Do you have a preference?"

"Maybe Italian, soon as I wash my hands."

"Sounds good," Solarin says. "And of course he's seen something."

"Who, Earl?"

"Yeah, he's probably seen lots of things."

"I mean," Lamb clarifies, "Things related to the case."

"Hmph," is all Solarin manages. He likely has more to say but bites his tongue out of respect for his junior partner.

Lamb quickly changes the subject. "Why do men like Gamble get to walk when they're clearly neck deep in it?"

Solarin ponders a moment like a father about to dish out some wisdom to his child at bedtime. "Usually, it's not so clear. Even men like Gamble can surprise you. Live long enough, and you come to realize there must be an opposition in *all* things . . . or this whole flea circus falls. You do realize Earl won't be there tomorrow."

Lamb draws a deep breath. "Yes I do."

$$15$$

Chapter Fifteen

Wendell rushes down the steps to the lobby, passes reception with unknown purpose before anyone can acknowledge him, and exits through the hotel's main doors. He steps from sidewalk to curb to asphalt, and on past the fountain and entry drive lined with palm tree sentinels toward the highway. He runs with purpose away from the central tower, his gaze floating over the road.

Without looking for oncoming traffic, he crosses to the other side. Luckily, he's not hit. Even if he were, she'd be worth it. There is only *her*. Straight ahead. That moving whisp of black. Her cloak that draws him onward. Ever onward. Into nowhere, that desolate western desert of nothingness.

Step-by-step he follows her.

After some time, he slows, but continues to press forward. He walks and walks, and the bleak desert stretches out before him like the setting of a dark fairytale. But as unwelcoming as the landscape seems, that fluttering cloak of Ava's welcomes him all the more over the dirt and scant desert grass and sagebrush. The plants themselves seem to whisper, egging him on. The warm afternoon air seems to cool, alive with its own energy and heartbeat.

The further he travels, the grayer it becomes, until it seems he's wandered into a poem by Edgar Allan Poe. It's as if the world slowly sucks back all its color—a bit more with each breath, with each step—leaving a complete void of saturation, with only a few notable exceptions: Ava's bright red corset under that dark cloak, her gown, and lips.

He draws closer, yearning to catch up, dying to reach her. And he suddenly realizes the desert has become a vast cemetery dotted with leafless trees and headstones. And cawing ravens. Lots of ravens.

Ava watches him closely. She speaks to him, but her words are only echoes on the casual breeze. Wendell and Ava have both stopped walking, but still the starkly surreal scenery moves beneath them.

Church bells chime, and everything in Wendell's field of vision wavers and distorts as if viewed in a curved mirror. His condition begins to assume threatening forms, as though he's tripping on LSD, and he sees beyond what's actually there.

One gravestone stands out above the rest. The grave itself is an empty rectangular hole before him, dug and ready to receive a coffin. It too morphs with his thoughts and swaying vision. And with hers.

Ava beckons to him with those delicate hands crowned with sharp red fingernails, and he moves to embrace her, but the ground beneath him gives way. He falls into the hole and rolls back onto his feet.

The gravestone beyond the hole is utterly blank, void of any name, dates, or quotations. It's a clean slate of polished stone, waiting to be carved.

Ava looks down at Wendell longingly from the edge, her cloak billowing in a sudden gust of wind. "Were you expecting to see something else?" Her voice seems a muffled echo, as does his own.

"To be honest, I was half expecting to see "Ebenezer Scrooge" engraved on the headstone."

She smiles, but there's no humor there.

It begins to rain. A light patter at first. Just enough to keep the dust down.

Wendell attempts to climb out of the pit, grasping at hanging roots and divots in the thickening mud. It proves a steep and difficult climb, slippery and mucky, but he manages to make it out with much effort. He realizes he's a sodden mess, a soiled clump at Ava's feet, and all he can do is stare up at her, defeated and ashamed.

She makes no immediate judgement, only offers him a hand to help

him to his feet.

"Thank you, Ava," he says, breathing hard.

"Oh Wendell. Why did you come here . . . so unprepared?"

The rain intensifies, until it becomes a deluge.

Wendell swallows. "What do you mean?"

She looks past him. "They only want you to feel welcome. But I—"

Wendell shakes his head. "You what?"

She stares off into the distance. "The voices. Do you hear them?"

"Who?" Wendell asks. "What voices?"

"They're calling you." A deep sense of melancholy laces her tone. "From far away they call."

Wendell steps back, nearly falling again into the mire. "What do they want, Ava?"

The pouring rain drenches them both, and lightning cracks across the grumbling sky. A million worms squirm their way out of the ground immediately around them. A thousand ravens leave their perch on distant trees and swarm. Gravestones shudder and slide on their foundations, and the dead claw their way through thick and stubborn sod.

Ava looks at him again. "Wake up."

"I don't want to wake up."

Deafening thunder shakes the uneven ground, and lightning strobes against her wet face. *That lovely face.*

"Wake up, Wendell . . . *WAKE UP!*"

She startles him.

"Wake up!"

Her screaming becomes a whisper, and then a chorus of whispers. And inside each voice lurks a strange sense of patronizing levity.

"*Welcome . . . Welcome, Wendell . . . Welcome . . . to the Hotel California.*"

Wendell rises on his elbows, drenched in his own sweat. He can feel his heartbeat in his head, neck, and chest. He breathes heavily, glancing down at the bedsheets softly molded over his torso, legs, and feet.

Eventually his breathing normalizes, and he peers out the all-too-familiar window of his assigned room. Nightmares containing dreams and dreams that give way to nightmares. One after the other. Night after night. Experience after experience. Had he taken the red handkerchief from Leo? Ingested what was inside? Had he accepted the psychedelic gift? Or was this all just another play of fate bouncing him back inside the walls of this hellish oasis?

He can't quite accept what he already knows the answer to be. He can't bring himself to think it. Not with absolution. And he sure as hell can't bring himself to call it what it is, *real* or *imagined*. Not at once. *This limbo. This purgatory. This*— "Damn you, Ava. Damn this . . . *prison.*"

In truth, I'm tripping in some alleyway in downtown Los Angeles, he tells himself. *I'm face down on that beloved avocado carpet at the base of my couch. I ate too much at the café. Had too much to drink at the bar. I went to a local party where someone slipped me a psychedelic or hallucinogen. Thought it would be funny. That would explain these extreme disassociations from reality.* He swallows the bile burning his throat, forcing it back down. He heads for the bathroom, relieves himself, drowsily throws on some clothes, and runs out of his godforsaken hotel room—*again*—if only just to talk to someone.

* * *

After tossing her Styrofoam leftovers container, Lamb stares at the crime scene photos she's studied a dozen times before: Mr. Whitmore's cold dead face peering up into oblivion from the floor of the back alley. The blood and detritus surrounding his body. The dumpsters and searched garbage bags, along with their itemized contents. The walls. The sidewalks. And then on to the snapshots of Kenneth Phillips, hanging there in that New York apartment like Marley's ghost.

"Angelo Rossi, mob boss," she whispers to herself, shifting in her uncomfortable seat at her LA field office desk. "Gallo family. Tom De Luca, the record promoter." She pauses to look up. "De Luca," she repeats, mentally noting to make another attempt at finding and questioning him. He was supposedly local. Solarin was probably already on it. She'd ask him soon as he got back from the toilet.

She returns to the gruesome photos.

Paper trails, receipts, and witness reports . . . and these photos of the bloody crime scenes. None of it explained the whereabouts of Jeremy Bianchi or Wendell Meyers, who'd both gone missing. "Joseph Gamble." She frowns, looking a dozenth time at the blood spatter and background details of each photo. Personal effects, accounting documents, business reports, the ledgers. They needed an eyewitness to talk.

She recalls one of the FBI photo lab's analysis techniques, identifying blue jeans by the pattern on their seams. Although used principally in bank robbery cases, matching denim pants by the light and dark patches or 'wear marks' along their seams has its merits as they create, effectively, a barcode that is unique to each pair. Although this method does contain several serious flaws in reliability, including seams on different pairs of jeans are often highly similar, and separately, multiple pictures of the same pant seam, taken under varying conditions, can appear starkly different from one another, it remains worth considering, be it with reasonable caution.

An array of similar techniques to assert matches for clothes, vehicles, human faces, and skin features also proves helpful in some cases, however, the people present in these photos are obviously not in the habit of donning denim, only designer suits. And the lack of vehicles in these photos also proves no help at all. That only leaves her with faces and skin features of others.

She squints at the out-of-focus backgrounds of each black-and-white photo. She ditches the pile from Phillip's file and goes back to re-examine Whitmore's. Turning away from the fence and dumpsters in the images, she focuses more on the angles facing the street, the shots taken facing away from where the body was found. She flips through the photos one-by-one looking for background figures, people on the street, passersby, *anyone*.

Of course, the FBI has its issues with image analysis echoed in earlier controversies over other forensic techniques. The bureau's lab technicians and scientists had long testified in court that they could determine what fingertip left a print and which scalp grew a hair to the exclusion of all others. Research and exonerations by forensic analysis have repeatedly disproved those claims, and the U.S. Department of Justice would likely no longer permit its forensic scientists to make such unequivocal statements.

FBI examiners often analyze low-quality images from bureau photographers or rare security camera footage, and it is reasonable to expect that the reliability of this technique may degrade under real-world imaging conditions, but still there was some sticking power in photographic evidence.

Lamb scrutinizes each photo, especially those with living, breathing bodies in the background (not dressed as law enforcement), and zeroes in her search. Two particular photos stand out, so she sets the others aside.

"Who do we have here?" she whispers, pulling a magnifying glass out of her drawer, and focusing on a few tiny figures at street level by the alley. Only one is looking toward camera.

She remembers being there, the newspapers, animal feces, condoms, and other debris. The putrid stench drifting up from storm drains.

Most of the figures she can't make out, are mere silhouettes, or with heads out of frame, except one on the second of the two candidate photos she now analyzes. A man seated against a brick wall. It looks to be a vagrant. A homeless man.

Mistakes in these identifications are costly, sometimes resulting in an innocent person being accused or sentenced and a guilty person walking free, so she must be sure.

She drops the magnifying glass, then looks through it again.

"Pareidolia," she says, eyeing the man's face through the magnifying lens.

She recognizes him. She gave him five bucks.

"Earl."

16

Chapter Sixteen

Having searched the city high and low, called around, and interviewed Earl's fellow vagrants, Agent Lamb begins to think her possible eyewitness may have packed his bags and relocated. She wanders into the city park as a last-ditch effort to find and follow-up on her one final lead. She walks over and collapses onto a nearby park bench, and watches two young boys playing near the pond. Joggers pass her by. People walking their dogs barely pay her notice.

Something like an hour later, Solarin strolls up next to her. "Did you expect to find him feeding the birds for tuppence a bag?"

"No," she says cooly, glancing up at him. "But I hoped."

"Ah, your first mistake. Don't worry, the job will soon take that out of you." He sighs and takes a seat next to her.

"That's not exactly true. Is it?" She looks off in the distance.

Solarin breathes deeply. "No, I suppose not. The job will make you jaded—if it hasn't already—un-trusting, skeptical. For some, even dirty—I'm sure you've seen it. One doesn't have to look too far. But there's the other side too. Look at the morning light splashing over those trees, glinting in the water. The children playing. Every time I look at my own kids. I joke, but there's still a God in Heaven that put all this in motion, wants us home . . . And he's asked us to hope."

"Well damn, I think you chose the wrong profession, Agent Solarin. I'd attend your Sunday services."

Solarin smiles and pats Lamb on the shoulder. You're too kind. *Too kind. Halleluiah,* heh heh."

Lamb grins back at him until the reality of their case eventually settles back in and changes the mood.

"You've checked the soup kitchens?" Solarin asks.

Lamb nods.

"Skid Row?"

"Yep. Briefly. Feared for my life."

"Yeah. Third Street? Seventh? Alameda? Main?"

"Yes, all the borders. No Earl."

Solarin sighs. "Wish you'd taken me with you to Central City East. You've been busy."

"Yes, I have. And you've gone through all the paperwork for the ump-teenth time?"

Solarin drops his head in the affirmative.

"So what's next? Shall we close it down? Write our final reports? Add it to the trove of unsolved mysteries?"

"Perhaps," Solarin says, nodding. "Most likely. Heaven knows—as do our superiors—we've spent too long on this case already. Assistant Director's already threatened to pull the plug at least twice, and I'm certain the SAC's been on his ass. Gamble's not talkin'. His lawyers are stonewalling."

"'Course they are."

The two little boys at the pond are called away by their mother, and they run off out of sight to meet her.

"You think they'll still let us work together?" Lamb asks.

Solarin exhales sharply. "Don't know." He looks her in the eye. "I *hope* so."

* * *

The question of what drives a man to gamble plays over Wendell's thoughts as he enters the in-house hotel casino, his potent self-awareness driving him to the utter brink of madness. But at the very least, there would be others here with which to associate. In popular culture over the

decades, winning at the tables was always connected with ideas of success, happiness, and a better life. The overt motivation: a simple desire to win money.

However, Wendell *has* money. Lots of it. He has felt the worldly successes for long enough, even short glimpses of happiness now and again. Then why can't he seem to grasp a better life or a happiness of the *lasting* kind? For years, he's tried, dabbling in this and that, eating world-class cuisine, drinking many of the finest drafts, dating here and there (sans any *real* commitment).

What motivates someone to gamble? Lots of things. But for Wendell, here, now?

He wants to say it's *hope*, but alas, it's merely *distraction*. After all, what does he have left to lose to this place?

Only his *money*.

It immediately becomes clear that blackjack, poker and pretty much every variation of casino game one can imagine are available to customers staying at the Hotel California. And there are plenty of signs that announce their availability 24/7. Roulette—the quintessential casino game—is also offered here, with huge sums of currency just waiting to rest on the spin of a wheel. One of the most exciting games in Wendell's not entirely inexperienced opinion. Quite different from the scorching party scene island of pools, bars, and cabanas outside, this vast, dimly lit space bathed in deep reds, golds, and browns, and colorfully eye-catching, cash-sucking machines lends an air of a slightly more discreet seduction. Gray clouds of billowing smoke from the tips of cigars and cigarettes ascend to and hover at the high, ornate ceiling, and they burn the nostrils. Bells ring, levers sound, pool balls break, and conversation creates a quiet noise that permeates the whole of the hall. The room has obviously long been a haunt for eager tourists or unexpecting travelers such as Wendell. And, of course, drinkers.

How much money would he spend here? What would be a reasonable cap for likely losses? What expenditures would be justifiable to hang on to his dangling string of sanity just a little bit longer? *Ever the accountant,* he broods, *even in my drunken stupors.*

Overall, the casino is elegant if time worn. It's not crowded, but a reasonable number of gamblers meander throughout. *So, this is where everyone comes when they're not getting sloshed on the pool deck.*

He approaches several banks of slot machines to his left and right. *Slots are for losers,* he thinks, passing them by. The brooding accountant means to try his luck at the tables first.

Wendell spies several games in progress, so he finds an open one, and grabs a seat.

Blackjack.

The dealer greets him with a winning smile, and Wendell places $500 cash over the betting spot printed on the cloth. The dealer shuffles and converts his money to gaming chips.

Wendell knows a skilled blackjack player has an almost even chance of winning against the house. Theoretically, out of every 100 hands played, the house wins 55 against a skilled player, but the cards don't know that so many times one can win considerably more games than they lose.

The cards are dealt. Red King and a six against the dealer's ten. Wendell's deflated. Hard sixteen. *Not a good start.* "Can I surrender?"

"I'm sorry, sir."

"Hit."

Another six. And the dealer flips to reveal a one-eyed Jack.

"Beginner's bad luck."

The dealer grins at the comment.

Wendell's chips are whisked away. He pushes more in.

A dark figure, silhouetted by a flashy marque pauses to watch Wendell from across the way. He wears a designer suit and a Homburg dress hat, his face obscured by shadow.

"Who is that?" Wendell asks, leading with his eyes.

The dealer doesn't even have to look. "That's the night man."

"Who's the night man?"

"You know," the dealer says, finishing the next shuffle, "House manager."

Frozen in place, the shadowed man seems interested in not only what's going on with the tables, but in Wendell himself. But it's more a feeling from his mere silhouette than anything tactile. An unsettling sensation.

Another ten for the dealer against a pair of eights. Wendell splits to improve his odds and gets hit with a nine versus the dealer's Ace.

"How long you worked here?" Wendell asks.

"Quite some time," he says.

Wendell goes in again and loses, nineteen versus twenty. Again. Twenty-three versus nineteen. Again. Twenty-four versus twenty. Again. Seventeen versus twenty-one.

"Dammit." Wendell tips the dealer and moves off, huffing. "Not my game."

"Very sorry, sir." The dealer's voice fades behind him.

Pulling out another wad of cash, Wendell wanders over to the Roulette tables. He finds an open spot and places his $300 worth of bets on red and a dozen random numbers.

The dealer, a blonde woman much older than Ava, spins the ball on the outer rim of the wheel, and it dances around before eventually falling into black six. Wendell's chips are quickly taken. He bets on red and those same numbers another five times, and he loses another $1,500.

Between this and his failures at the Blackjack table, never had he gambled away such an amount in so short a time. Money he could afford to lose, but a hit to his pride that could push him to the brink. Wendell grabs onto the sides of the table, as if for balance or emotional support. His knees struggle to lift him to his feet as he stands and staggers away. The air itself seems to deflate his lungs, and a huge unseen weight like an invisible python constricts his chest.

"Are you alright?" asks the dealer with a slight of concern, her voice only a muffled echo.

Wendell raises a half-cocked arm and betrays his true feelings with a nod.

He shakes off the dysphoria and finds his balance against a nearby pillar, resting for several long minutes, attempting to forget the devastating losses. Reaching deep to find whatever grit remains within, Wendell looks up with determination and enters the velvet-roped salle privee at the center of the grand space. *To hell with games of chance and bad hands.* He would rely on his skill in reading the other players at a classic hand of poker.

Of course, Leo is there, the only one he recognizes. Why wouldn't he be? "Small world," says the old man as Wendell steps past and joins the other three who sit by the dealer.

"And it's getting smaller," Wendell replies, taking a seat. Even Leo's voice is an echo.

The dealer, eyes on his hands, says, "Game is no limit Texas hold'em, five communal cards, two in the hole, minimum stake five thousand."

Wendell opens his wallet, and realizes he's already blown all his cash.

"We can spot you the chips," says the dealer. "We have your information at the front desk, and we have collectors."

Wendell nods, returning his wallet to his back pocket, and glances at the other players. A middle-aged businessman, an elegant older woman with a super-cropped Flapper Bob haircut in black, a balding heavyset gentleman in a rattlesnake suit, and Leo.

"Have you all been waiting for me?" Wendell asks, trying to hold it together.

They all look at him as he receives several hefty stacks of chips, but no one answers.

"How nice."

"Shall we begin?" asks the dealer, shuffling.

Wendell gives a go-ahead and cuts the cards.

Ava strides up from behind Wendell wearing a diamond crested bra, G-string, sparkly angel wings, and an ornate headdress of small white feathers. She gently rests a hand on his shoulder, momentarily distracting him, as two other girls in like dress join her to watch the game.

"Didn't know you were a showgirl," Wendell says. "Is there a theater here?"

"'Course there is," she says. "And I prefer *dancer.*"

"Noted." Wendell suddenly realizes just how little he knows about this woman, infatuation or not. It does, however, explain her indefinite boarding situation in the middle of nowhere, and Wendell certainly wouldn't want to miss her stage performance. Presently, it's his turn.

The cards are dealt face-down.

Rather than examine his own hand, Wendell looks for reactions from the other players. Leo grins back at Wendell, but no-one else gives anything away.

Wendell notices the night man's silhouette standing next to the slot machines. He's further away than before but remains fixed in his direction.

The game commences.

The businessman, first to have a bet, folds.

"Ten thousand," says the woman.

Rattlesnake suit nods and matches her bet, concealing all emotion.

Wendell glances down at his cards, all too aware of everyone's eyes upon him. *Two black Aces.*

"Ten thousand." Wendell returns their stares.

Leo, to his right, folds.

The dealer lays down the flop and, as the others view the three community cards, Wendell's focus is on the others' reactions to them.

The businessman is neutral. Disappointment shows on the woman's face, almost imperceptibly.

Leo and Ava watch Wendell as his gaze shifts to the bald man in the snake suit, who studies him in turn.

Wendell lets slip a smile as he looks down at the flop. Three diamonds: nine-eight-five.

The businessman knocks, as does the woman. Rattlesnake watches Wendell and says, "Twenty-five thousand."

There is an audible reaction. Wendell eyes the bald man. He must have a flush or three-of-a-kind to be playing so strong. Or he's bluffing.

The right side of his mouth lifts ever so slightly, and he clears his throat to mask it.

Wendell pushes in twenty-five thousand to match, which brings an even bigger reaction.

Things escalated fast.

The businessman and Flapper Bob throw away their cards.

The dealer drops 'the turn,' the next common card. Again, Wendell initially watches Rattlesnake's reaction over the card.

It's a nine.

Rattlesnake purses his lips.

A pair out in the open, like fangs. Could Rattlesnake have the other nines? Not that it matters, as Wendell's already decided to go all the way and discover if the serpent's mouth contained the tell.

The bald man bets. "Fifty thousand."

Wendell glances over at Ava, her glittering breasts at his eye level. She looks down at him with a worried expression. He desperately wants his actions to show he's doughty in the face of difficulty, but only persistence can show his bravery now. *Bravery or stupidity.*

"Good luck, Wendell," she says, her eyes betraying her tone.

He just wants to get lost in Ava's bosoms, but must face this hand, this opponent, this pit of vipers. How could he have wandered into this situation willingly? And dropped all this money? Why would he want to talk to *these* people?

Ava backs away a step or two, mirroring his own wishes.

The bald man impatiently shuffles his cards.

"... Mr. Meyers?" says the dealer.

Had he told the dealer his name? "Yes, of course. Sorry." Wendell matches Rattlesnake's bet, the inner accountant screaming in protest.

'The river,' the last card is dealt. Everyone watches it except Wendell and Rattlesnake, who watch each other.

Two of diamonds. Rattlesnake breathes deeply, puffing out his chest. The mouth, a flat line, wholly still. "One hundred thousand."

Everyone at the table or watching from the sidelines, is mesmerized.

The accountant has left the building. Wendell pushes in a hundred thousand. "Call."

The Rattlesnake stares back at him.

The dealer turns to the bald man. "Sir, you have been called."

The Rattlesnake shows his cards: black two's.

"That's a full house," says the dealer, turning to Wendell. "And you sir?"

Wendell sinks in his chair, sick to his stomach, and throws his cards on the table.

A momentary hush that sucks the air out of the room, and the bald man rakes in his chips.

Wendell plays five more rounds, and loses every time, twice to the woman, once to the businessman, and a second time to rattlesnake suit.

"That does it." The triumphant bald man eyes Wendell as he gathers his winnings yet again. "Maybe gambling's not your thing."

"You might want to stop by the desk," says the dealer, "To make arrangements for your debt."

A flood of shock and embarrassment envelopes Wendell. And it isn't even about the money. Could he afford to lose it? Not an easy or clear-cut question to answer at the moment.

"I don't usually—" He looks back at Ava, sees the utter disappointment in her eyes—or is it pity? —and quickly looks away. "Forgive me. I—I don't—"

"It's okay," she says. "Everyone loses."

"Everyone? *Every* game?" A sudden migraine surfaces, and he grasps his forehead. He pushes off from the table, and stumbles from the platform, catching his balance on the arm of a waiter, causing them to drop their tray and spill several drinks on the floor.

"Hey!"

"Sorry. My apologies. Please, just—"

Wendell staggers through the casino, the buzz and echo of everyone's voices filling his ears with a building pressure that needs to pop. A hellish chorus of bells, whistles, billiard balls cracking, raising in volume, and the whole place goes corybantic. However, Wendell can't decide if the wild and frenzied atmosphere is happening around him or within. The smoke and smells grow seedier, more rank than before. The laughter of others now seems aimed at him and intensified. *Only* him. And his view of the world distorts, the colorful conglomeration of images becoming skewed through a glass darkly yet vividly disturbing.

A dark presence like that felt when first setting eyes on the night man seems to rest over his shoulders like a black predatory beast. One that presses him forward, onward, out of the casino and toward the closest flight of stairs.

Ava calls after him from behind, but he can't let her see him now. Not like this. Not as the *loser.*

Physically, he ascends throughout the building—floor by floor—while mentally, he spirals downward. Ever downward. Wendell coughs and sputters, spittle foaming on his lips like that of a rabid animal. How much did he have to drink? What else did he take? How could it have come to this?

Huffing, he reaches the top floor, and he frantically searches for a fire escape or corner stairwell. He needs fresh air. He needs out of this place. These . . . walls of claustrophobia. He needs . . .

"Yes." Down the long hallway, he sees a door with the words: "Roof Access – Authorized Personnel Only."

He makes for the escape, fully expecting the door to be locked. It isn't. He bursts through and climbs a mounted ladder across the small custodial closet, exiting through a roof access hatch into the cool breeze of night.

He collapses onto the gravel from the raised trapdoor as the panel falls shut, and he crawls to the edge of the building, dragging himself up over the wall to peer down at the fluorescent, cherry red marque and the hotel entry drive lined with palms that sway in the wind.

It's a relatively clear night with a sky full of stars and a small crescent moon, but Wendell's head couldn't be more muddled.

Tears stream down his face. His hands and feet tremble. So many doubts cast a nubilous blanket over his ability to reason, and his body spasms like it wants to eject everything it's taken in. Gripping the ledge, Wendell drags his body up onto the lip, rolling on his back to face the dark heavens above, until he's parallel with the massive majuscule sign fourteen stories up. A mere meter to the gravel rooftop and AC units at his left, and a terminal freefall to concrete by those gaudy aureate doors to his right. "Good luck, collectors."

He simply can't take any more of this hellish nightmare; he cannot keep reliving failure after failure. And he can't keep ending up on his own. *How could a hurtbag like me ever have a beauty like Ava anyway? Or a life that would warrant it?*

He weeps. And still, he can hear their whispers. *"Welcome. Welcome, Wendell. Welcome . . . to the—"* He can't take it anymore. He's got to get the voices out of his head.

"God, forgive me."

Squeezing his eyes shut, he rolls to his right.

He hits the sign, causing *"Hotel California"* to flicker, and he flips and plummets to the violent impact of the sidewalk fourteen stories below.

17

Chapter Seventeen

Lamb spills her coffee on the white tablecloth, some of it splashing and steaming against the side of her hand. "Ouch!"

"You alright?" Solarin reaches from across the table and grabs an extra napkin for her.

She shakes her head. "Yeah, just—"

"You uh, you were saying?" Solarin hands her the cloth.

"Yes, thanks. I was going to say, Meyers is either dead in a ditch somewhere or mocking us, living a life of luxury completely and utterly off-grid. Maybe Bianchi too. I was about to call it. Er . . . let *you* call it." She flashes a grin.

"So what made you keep looking for this guy, Earl? I mean, the displaced are ghosts, especially when law enforcement takes an interest. And the bowery? Skid Road's no joke. Why didn't you call me?"

Lamb's eyebrows raise as she thinks of her return to the ghetto in search of the man who is presently taking a bathroom break in the back of the corner night café.

"When I first visited LA as a girl, heading south on I-5 in the back of my parent's station wagon, I remember seeing the edge of the skyline appear. Buildings made famous from popular films were clearly visible against the sky. I can still see the wisps of cirrus clouds. Out the back window I watched people encamped beneath the overpasses and a few more spread out along the underbrush that bordered the thoroughfares. I remember saying to my parents, "There are so many here. Is this it?"

"No," my dad said. "This is the outskirts."

"We drove past a spot right off 7ᵗʰ Avenue, and as we made our way downtown, we moved through streets lined with blue tarps that looked like they would be more appropriate in a recreational park. Then it dawned on me: This was a campsite and the colorful tarps I saw were tents—*homes*—for the people living here. We must have passed several hundred of them on just the first few blocks. Most were packed tightly, marked territories, boundaries between living habitations each not much wider than a parking space."

Solarin nods thoughtfully, obviously aware of the scene, which hadn't really changed much over the years.

"Against my mom's wishes," Lamb continues, "My dad stops the car and gets out. There's a noise that sounds like a lawnmower backfiring. My mom tells me to lock the doors, so I do. Someone across the street is running—a woman. And then others start running, screaming. It's all the homeless near a concentrated encampment. Everyone starts making noise. I turn and see smoke rising, and then flames. It's a big fire."

Lamb takes pause as she thinks back on it. "There was a man. As I recall, he looked a little like you, though not quite as handsome." She tries to smile through her gathering tears. "He was on fire. Running. Screaming. Rolling. Very close to the car."

She lets out a heavy exhale. "I just sat there and watched from behind my window with my mom. I'd never seen anything like it, not even on TV."

"And your dad?" Solarin asks with genuine interest.

"My dad tried to help the man, rolled him on the ground. Problem was, the man's clothes were soaked in vodka, and he was burned bad. Even my dad's arm caught fire as he tried to help him. Got second-degree burns all up and down his arms."

"And the homeless man?"

Lamb shakes her head. "We took him to the hospital, but he didn't make it ... My dad tried to wrap him in a blanket, but I could still see his charred flesh. I can still remember the smell."

Solarin looks down at his clasped hands.

"All for some meaningless boundary dispute between vagrants." Lamb takes a sobering drink.

"Yeah, it happens," Solarin says.

"But I also noticed that many of those people showed genuine concern. They cared for him. They care for one another. *Truly care.* And they're observant. City's best surveillance system. They got eyes just about everywhere."

"Right . . . so—"

"So, when I was searching for Earl the first time, I thought as I walked along the streets, I can see the sense of community here—or rather small pockets within these nomadic groupings. There seems to be a comfortable sensibility that lay beneath the outer volatile veneer. There are rules which are understood, and a status hierarchy based upon mores with which I'm either unfamiliar or afraid to discover."

"And . . .?"

"I wondered where new arrivals are housed or if the anonymous governing bodies segregate the immigrants. I think Earl's an immigrant, thus his being there at SkyBox that day rather than Skid Row. And I thought, there must be some way his movement can be dictated or at least, understood. I was certain that to set up in any open spot would recruit an uncomfortable punishment. Dressed like this, that is. FBI, police, detectives, we draw too much attention. I'm sure there's a process for being exiled either from this LA township, or for more serious transgressions, from planet Earth."

"So the next time you went back to question people about Earl's process." Solarin smiles.

Lamb beams. "But dressed like *them*."

"You know, I would like to have seen that." Solarin leans back on his bench and stretches. "Earl's been in there a while."

Lamb looks up at Solarin with a sudden concern, having lost track of time. "Yeah, *too* long."

Instead of making for the men's room, she bursts through the doors onto the street outside the café. She sees a small open window at the outer wall of the men's restroom in the back, and peers down each connected crossroads, again trying to put herself in Earl's shoes.

She chooses a direction and starts running. Solarin sees her and takes a different route.

Her feet pounding over pavement, Lamb soon spies the hobbling form of a man in brown rags dragging a bag of belongings between streetlights. "Earl! Stop! What are you doing? Stop!"

The homeless man continues to try and get away, but he's no match for Lamb on foot.

She eventually catches up to him and holds him fast, exasperated. "Earl," she huffs, breathing though her mouth so she doesn't have to smell him. "What the hell are you doing?! You agreed to talk with me, and I agreed to buy you a hot meal and put you up in a nice place for a month, give you some spending money. Right? Do you remember? Geez!"

With dirty face, he glances back at her sheepishly. "Yes, yes, I'm sorry. Sorry, Maggie. You know, your partner, he . . . he spooked me. I suppose I got spooked."

"My partner is a teddy-bear," Lamb says, turning Earl around and walking him back in the direction of the café with a firm hand on his shoulder. "You should, however, be afraid of *me* after pulling a stunt like this."

Earl chuckles. "Yeah, ha, ha. Afraid."

"How'd you fit through that window anyway? And with your bag?"

"I chucked it out first," he says deviously.

"I see."

"Yeah." He laughs.

"So what's it going to be, Earl?"

"Wh-What do you mean?"

"Steak, potatoes? Soup, salad? Or are you more of a *cheeseburger* guy?"

"With a drink?" he asks.

"A soda," says Lamb.

"Oh, I dunno then." Earl grins and giggles, and hobbles along with her, dreaming up his order.

"Or better yet, water." She says. "And then a bath."

Solarin finally spots his partner and the vagrant and meets up with them on the street, despite the poor lighting of the area. "Hello, Earl. Thought you might grab some fresh air?"

"You know it, *FBI*."

Solarin smiles shallowly, and escorts them back to the café, back to their table.

Sitting across from him, they let the man order and enjoy the better part of his meal before bringing up the case.

Lamb starts, "Earl, I mentioned earlier that we'd have some questions for you."

"FBI always have questions," Earl says, eyeing them both from behind his French fries, which he smothers in ketchup and eats two at a time. "You never run out of them."

Lamb smiles as he licks his fingers and sips his soda through a straw. "That's true—"

"You could say," Earl continues, obviously thinking he's clever, "That your job is—"

"To ask questions," Lamb finishes the thought, "Yep, that's the cliché."

"So, Earl," Solarin says, clearly wanting to get on with it, but Lamb stops him with a soft hand over his.

"Earl," Lamb says with a motherly tone, "That day outside the SkyBox investment firm where we first met, you said you saw *dangerous* things."

Earl stops chewing, and he squeezes the two fries in his greasy fingers. "Yes." He looks down, as if regretful. "Yes, dangerous. Dangerous things."

"What happened?" Lamb asks. "Take your time. Think back. What happened on the street that day?"

Earl shakes his head. "Wasn't on the street."

"What do you mean?"

Earl looks up at her, and their eyes connect. "Didn't happen on the street. Happened in the back."

"In the back of the building?"

Earl nods, his face, haunted.

"Behind the alley?" Lamb presses. "By the dumpsters? Employee parking?"

"Yeah, in the back," Earl says.

"Okay. What happened?"

"That's where they brought out the bodies." Earl pushes his plate of remaining fries away and moves on to a plate of toast, slapping strawberry

jam over the first slice with a butter knife.

Lamb and Solarin exchange glances.

Lamb puts a gentle hand on Earl's arm, and he freezes. "Whose bodies, Earl?"

He just sits there a moment, frozen in time, then shrugs. "Suits."

"Suits?" Solarin asks.

Earl nods. "Fancy pants."

"Did you recognize them?" Lamb asks.

He shakes his head. "Just suits. Rack and jacks."

Lamb nods. "Okay, good. How many, Earl? How many bodies?"

"Two." Earl takes his first bite, and strawberry jam escapes down the sides of his mouth and beard.

"Alright, this is helpful. Who carried the bodies out of the building?"

Earl thinks a moment. "Big guys."

"Were they wearing suits too?"

Earl shakes his head. "No. *Big* guys. One was like a . . . a truck driver. Or uh, an oil rig operator. Somethin' like that."

"Were they like *mob* guys?"

Earl shakes his head, waving a hand. "Oh no, no. I don't mess with that. Them's some *bad* guys."

"Right," Lamb says. "Earl, this next question is very important. I need you to think carefully before answering."

"Yeah okay. Shoot."

"Where did they take the bodies? What did they do with them?"

He takes another bite of toast and chews, thinking, his chin slathered.

"Did they put them in a car?" Lamb asks. "A van? Where did you see this from?

Earl shakes his head. "Broken fence."

"Through a broken fence?"

"Yeah, they uh, they had a cement truck."

"Cement truck? What do you mean?"

"New cement they was pourin'," Earl says. "In the back."

Lamb attempts to clarify: "Wait. They were pouring new concrete in the back of SkyBox?"

Earl shakes his head again. "Uh, no. Uh-uh."

"Where?" Solarin asks. "Where was this truck?"

Earl looks up at Solarin with irritation. "Where? Who? Too many questions. Just let me eat. Huh? Finish my damn meal first?"

"Sorry, Earl, but please. We're almost done here," Lamb says, taking the reins back from Solarin. "Where were they pouring the cement? This is *very* important."

He coughs and wipes at his face with his dirty sleeve. "Oh hell, I don't know. Couple buildings over, I guess."

"Did they dump the bodies, and cover them in the new concrete?"

Earl keeps quiet, and chews on the question, as though he's too ashamed to answer.

Lamb leans in. "Can you show us? Can you take us there, Earl?"

He looks up. "Do you think we could we maybe get another meal like this?"

"Sure."

Looking around, he hesitates, then nods. "Yeah, okay."

* * *

"You didn't think it was going to be that easy, did you?" A demonic voice stands out over the ringing in Wendell's ears.

Wendell lies face down on the concrete, hurt, but conscious. "Lord, help me," he whispers. "I'm so sorry. Sorry for everything. I need you . . . I need you *now*."

"He doesn't hear you, Wendell Meyers," comes the guttural, skeletal voice of a deep-throated man from behind. "He doesn't *see* you. Not here. Not even out of the corner of his eye."

The demon in a suit draws closer and leans in, his odor reeking of dead animal and his breath putrid. "But *I* see you."

"Get away. Go away!" Wendell strains and jumps to his feet, swatting violently at the black suit, and making for the doors.

The dark figure—whose silhouette Wendell now recognizes as the night man from the casino—chuckles at his attempt to flee, then slips a finger across the brim of his Homburg dress hat mockingly. "But where would I go?"

Wendell blinks, and the approaching emaciated face of the night man transforms, his menacing appearance suddenly becoming handsome. He's well-dressed in his designer suit, but something about the demon seems to challenge what plain sight paints as veridical. His sun-tanned complexion, dark hair and light blue eyes could even be considered attractive now. "You see, *here*, I can clean up as well as anyone."

"*I should be dead*," Wendell says, replaying his fall from the top of the main tower over in his mind.

"*Yes.*"

"I just want to go home."

"You *are* home." He walks forward, backing Wendell against the golden exterior doors.

"No. My life in LA."

"There is nothing for you in the City of Angels."

"My job. SkyBox."

The night man smiles. "Ah, yes, I'm afraid you've been terminated."

"Jeanine."

"Like you, she has also left the city."

"How do you know that?"

That disconcerting smile deepens. "We conduct diligent research on *all* our guests . . . as well as their known associates."

"My home, my car. *Friends.*"

"Your car is here, down in the garage, albeit broken—a passion project if you like. I already told you; this is your home now. And, Wendell, I hate to say this, but you don't have any friends. You've alienated them. Lost touch over the years. You became so obsessed with your work, your job, that they lost all importance in your life, and you know as well as I, they matter very little when it comes to your daily itinerary. You even stopped trying to make new ones. I mean, it truly does require a certain amount of energy and effort to foster a friendship, I'll give you that. A certain amount of selflessness, right? And besides, just look at all the friends you've made since your arrival here. Even the staff members consider our guests *friends.*"

"Just so you know, the politeness in this place is infuriating."

"Thank you for the input—we welcome constructive criticism. We shall take that into consideration and run it down the line."

"Who are you?"

The night man takes Wendell by the arm, and suddenly they are standing in his hotel room.

Wendell looks around, taken aback, wanders next to his bed, and falls to his knees. "Some new demon sent here to torment me?"

The night man chuckles icily. "No, no. I am no one new. You've known me well enough even since your arrival here. Long before, in fact. I am no mere fixture of this place, or an employee. I am no contrivance of your mind. And I am certainly no spirit come from the underworld. No . . . I *am* this hotel. Or at the very least, everything it represents."

Wendell just doesn't have the strength anymore. He drops his head low to the floor. "And what is that? The manager? Owner?"

"This is, shall I say, my party . . . and you are my guest. I am simply the night man. I am your *natural* man. I am everything your unfettered heart desires. I am all the fine things. The luxuries. The escapades. Your unbridled passions. The shimmering pool deck. The ballroom, its chandeliers, the suits, and oh so lovely evening gowns. Sweet debaucheries. Hedonism's halls. I reside behind the bar, ready to serve. I am inside the bottles. I throw lavish parties. And I am all the vices, even the ecstasies of retreat . . . I reside in the little red handkerchiefs."

Wendell's disbelieving eyes meet his.

The night man looks down at Wendell's crumpled form, almost with pity. ". . . *I am your lust for Ava.*"

"You're no such thing."

"Ah, well. Perhaps it's my new face that confuses you. Don't worry. We'll have plenty of time to get to know each other better. For you see, I am stuck here like you. And we have all the time in the world to become better acquainted."

"I'd rather be in prison."

"Oh, you are in prison. One of your own making, in fact."

Wendell begins to sob quietly, his tears and mucus seeping into the fibers of the stiff carpet.

"Just relax," he says in his condescending way. "Compose yourself, man. And take heart. Of course, here at the Hotel California we are programmed to receive the unwary or unwitting traveler. The destitute man. The gypsy. The banker. Those who have abandoned all inhibition. And if it is merely being stuck in one place that troubles you, worry not. You can roam around, do different things, as you have already discovered. And if it makes you feel better, you can check out at any time. Walk to the gas station if you feel up to it. See if the old man is still kicking around in the place."

Wendell casts his dreadful gaze up at the devil man.

The demon leers back at him. "Why yes. You may drop your room key at reception whenever you like . . ." He turns on his heel and walks confidently to the door but stops short and glances back. ". . . But then, I do suppose . . . you can never . . . actually . . . *leave*."

Wendell drops his head once again and continues to sob.

"Oh, and before I go, I must deliver the message I came here to deliver: We are preparing a dinner for you. A *special* dinner, to be held in your honor as our most recent guest."

"Most recent?" Wendell balks at the thought, trying to remember how long it's been since he checked in. "No one has arrived since—?"

"Our most recent guest," the night man repeats with emphasis. "Will you join us for this singular meal?"

Wendell doesn't answer.

"I do hope you will join us. We spared no expense. The master's suite. Nine o'clock or—to be honest—*whenever* you happen by." He turns to leave but pauses yet again. "And dress nice, you know . . . *for Ava*. There will be dinner *and* a show.

18

Chapter Eighteen

"You know, my mother is dead," says Earl to Agents Lamb and Solarin as they exit the Ford Galaxie and step over the curb toward an alleyway only a few blocks from SkyBox Investments & Asset Management Firm.

"I'm sorry to hear that," Lamb says, rubbing the sleep from her eyes, and glancing over at Solarin, whose idea it was to do this at 5 a.m., before too much traffic or too many pedestrians could interfere or get curious about their investigation. As she notices the empty sidewalks and scarce passing vehicles in what was normally busy downtown, her simmering resentment is dwarfed by the professionalism in his wise suggestion.

"Were you close with your mother?" Lamb asks the likely witness, whom she had forced to take a bath, brush his teeth, and don a brand-new set of clothes she herself had picked out and paid for, calling it a *gift*.

Solarin had teased her for growing a soft spot for the vagrant, but later apologized and complimented her generosity.

"She carried me in her belly," Earl says, "suffered through childbirth, raised me best she could. Isn't *everybody* close with their mothers?"

"*Maybe* . . . before they turn *twelve*. But good for you, Earl." She pats him on the back.

Solarin stands up straight, hands on his hips, breathing in the crisp, early-morning air, and gawks at the high-rises surrounding them. "So, Earl, where are we going today?"

Earl stops and looks around. "Maybe we could have b-breakfast."

"Earl," Lamb presses, "we discussed this. Work first, food later. Right? Don't you trust me?"

Earl looks down at his new comfortable loafers, but the man looks anything but comfortable. "Yes, but uh, I-I think we should eat. I think maybe—" He squats down on his haunches, stabilizing himself with a shaky hand on the ground.

Solarin watches the exchange, rolls his eyes, and drops his head, impatient with the man's hesitance to assist them. "Here we go," he mutters.

Lamb squats down before Earl and takes his hands in her own, meeting his eyeline. "Listen to me, Earl. We *need* you. We can't do this without you. Only *you* can show us where to find these missing people, bring them justice, peace. We need you to remember . . . and show us the place."

Letting out a trembling sigh, Earl's downcast eyes ultimately find their courage and look up through his dangling locks to see Lamb's reassuring gaze. She puts a helping hand on his shoulder and nods before standing and lifting. Slowly, he follows her lead.

"That's it," she says. "You can do this. You *must* do this."

Lamb appeals to Solarin with a look, and he steps forward, putting a commending arm around his junior partner.

Earl, mustering the nerve, stares at the alley ahead as though he were a knight, and a terrible dragon lurks just behind the back street lane, ready to consume him with fire.

"What's wrong?" Lamb says.

"N-nothing." He shuffles forward, his voice trailing.

"That's it," Lamb says.

"Okay," he utters. "Okay, Maggie."

"Yes." Her eyes soften.

Earl shrugs. "I think I-I remember . . . the place."

"That's great, Earl. Lead on—we're right here."

They enter a narrow, winding space, the walls, a massive, changing conglomeration of swatches between varying styles and colors of eroded brick. Wendell shuffles through the gap first, a familiar environment for someone in his nomadic housing situation.

Lamb and Solarin have his back as they advance through the seedy and enclosed cityscape. Metal piping winds up from the ground to the

B.C. Nailes

heights. Garbage and palettes are stacked up to barred windows and boarded-up garage doors with the occasional splash of graffiti or gang symbols over black paneling. Steam escapes here and there from ground-level vent covers and sewer drops to climb up the walls and escape into the slit of pink sky high above.

The agents, silent and observant, follow Earl toward the back, a significant distance away.

Earl whispers and mutters to himself as he shuffles along, but Lamb can't quite interpret his ramblings.

"What's he saying?" Solarin whispers to Lamb.

She shakes her head. "Don't know."

They approach a rusty and dilapidated fence which blocks off a quarter-acre courtyard to the left. Overgrown weeds, a tagged dumpster next to an abandoned shed, and two broken-down vehicles take up the perimeter of the forgotten space, but the center of the lot contains a flawless twelve-by-twelve-foot square pad of newly laid concrete.

Earl sees the spot through the chain-link, and immediately turns away, as if he's ashamed to even look.

Lamb and Solarin peer through the fence at the concrete slab and surrounding fenced-off area.

"Is that it?" Lamb asks. "Is this where you saw the cement truck a few weeks ago?"

Without facing them, Earl hunches and nods, hiding his head behind raised shoulders, "Mm-hm. Mm-hm." And he commences whispering incoherent mumblings.

Lamb blinks and straightens to her full stature. "We've got to get in there."

Solarin draws a long breath. "Yes, we do."

"We'll need a warrant."

He sighs. "Mm-hm."

They look around the fence for alternate entry points, of which there are none, then up at the coiled razor wire running along the top.

"Look at the fence," Lamb says. "*Old. Rusty. Dilapidated.* And the razor wire—"

"Brand-spankin' new." Solarin finishes her thought, pulling out a pair of utility pliers with a cutting edge.

They both start to climb. "Reasonable articulable suspicion, right?" says Solarin.

Lamb nods, remembering her training. "It's a gray area, but I'd lean toward suspect violation of law or regulation. In such case, entry into the property can be made, and it's not a trespass."

Solarin heaves and grunts. "But we *can* still get hurt . . . or attacked."

"Whoa, uh," Earl sees them out of the corner of his eye, "I wouldn't uh, do that . . . if I were you. Uh-uh. Be careful."

Gripping the chain-link with their fingers and tips of their shoes, Lamb and Solarin quickly scramble to the top, where they slow down to place their hands and feet more carefully, overtly mindful of their weight and points of impact, cautious to avoid the steel cutting barbs. Solarin cuts and pulls back the wire in a few places, which helps.

Even the coarse, unprotected wires and poles dig into the fleshy parts of their arms and hands, making the climb extremely uncomfortable.

"Easy," Solarin says sarcastically, grunting as he goes.

Lamb focuses on the task at hand; warily negotiating over the main coils, she finds a solid foothold, and leaps and rolls to the ground on the other side.

"Ouch!" Solarin whips his hand up and curses.

"Careful," says Lamb, examining her arms and legs. She has two small cuts on her lower legs, and her left forearm also bleeds where she had nicked the wire.

Solarin jumps down next to her with similar wounds. Wincing, he asks, "How'd *you* fair?"

"'Bout the same as you—couple of good slices. Don't suppose you have a first aid kit handy?"

"In the car."

Nursing their wounds with hand and sleeve, they make it to their feet and survey the enclosed area.

Earl steels a glance now and again from the other side of the fence, his nervous ticks taking over and escalating.

Besides the old fence and new security measures, Solarin and Lamb find fresh vehicle tracks, new locks on old gates, several fresh sets of footprints in the dried grass and dirt, and a locked and bolted door to the adjoining high-rise.

They both eventually gravitate back to the concrete slab in the center of the lot.

"We're going to need to pull this up," Solarin says, looking down past his feet.

Lamb too peers at the pad, wondering what—if anything—it contains. "Yeah."

"Where's Earl?" Solarin asks, suddenly glancing around.

Having neglected her side-viewing radar, Lamb looks back toward the fence and runs over to find him. Again, she peers up at the razor wire, and sighs. "He's gone."

Solarin joins her. "What happened to 'work first, eat later?'"

* * *

Wendell stands in the top floor hallway outside the corner master's suite, still like a wax figure, waiting for his date. No doors on this level open or close. Nobody comes or goes. Either he is very early to this 'special' dinner to be held in his honor, or very late. He hasn't eaten anything all day, and his stomach churns, but likely not for lack of food.

The elevator dings, startling him, and Ava steps up from behind, dressed to the nines in an elegant, simple-cut evening gown with almost translucent color. She carefully takes the arm of his blue and black jacket, almost like it's been rehearsed.

Wendell glances over at her. "You look beautiful." And she does. But he enjoyed spending time with her much more when he didn't know what this place was behind its glittering facade, when he didn't know the night man existed to oversee this prison of decadence. What he would give to be an ignoramus again.

"Thank you, handsome."

"You know," Wendell says as though it's a confession, "I had to call room service to bring me some wine, just to get myself to come."

"Oh yeah? What vintage?"

"First, I asked for Burgundy, but they said they haven't carried it since

S.C. HAILES

1969. So I went for Piedmont."

"Nice."

They both look ready for a stroll down the red carpet in lights, but almost instantly, the mood darkens.

"So what now?" Wendell asks. "Is it time?"

"Don't be alarmed," Ava says cryptically, peering cautiously down the hallway as though the 'pretty' boys from the pool party are ex-boyfriends, and they're waiting behind one of these doors to accuse her of cheating. But no, it's much worse. "*His* ubiquitous influence is felt by all in the family. Don't make the mistake of thinking you're alone."

"What do you mean?"

"Shhh."

The night man steps out from behind door number 1412, *Wendell's* room, into the hallway, smiling knowingly at Ava.

Wendell feels violated in some way, wondering if, as he was getting ready, the night man had already been there watching him from inside a closet or behind the bathroom door. He throws Ava a concerned look.

"He does that," she says.

Disquieted, Wendell follows her lead and steps forward beside her through the strange silence. Ava's tenseness and consistent tugging suggests the only answer to the night man's invitation is to accept.

"I need another drink," says Wendell.

"In good time." Ava squeezes his arm.

Before the night man can even say "Shall we?" or allow them to make it to the door, their surroundings change, and Wendell is already seated at the head of a long dinner table in a grand and beautiful dining hall. Men in tuxedos, women in gowns, some of whom he recognizes—even from his dream of the saloon—surround the elegant spread of goblets, wine bottles, and heaping platters of the finest culinary masterpieces.

"How did—?"

"Welcome, Wendell," says the night man, raising a glass from the opposite end of the table, "Welcome to the Hotel California."

Ava, just next to him, also raises a glass. And everyone else follows suit.

"Cheers!" They all exclaim in unison.

Wendell finds his own crystal goblet and raises it awkwardly a little too late. The potations of his college days are a bit blurry, but he's sure he hasn't joined as stroppy a toast since.

"There are mirrors on the ceiling," Wendell whispers to Ava as he glances around at the magnificent room.

"I know, right? There's even champagne on ice . . . and it's *pink*," she replies with a bob of her shoulders.

"Fancy."

The dinner commences, and delectable appetizers are passed around and enjoyed.

Hesitantly, Wendell ventures a small taste from each platter that comes his way and is rewarded with pleasantly stimulated taste buds.

If he's honest with himself, he's never tasted anything quite so exquisite.

And then, out of the blue, the night man launches into direct conversation with Wendell, notwithstanding the large room full of people. "So . . . *Wendell,* it has been said, there are only two kinds of men in this world: the righteous who think they are sinners and the sinners who think they are righteous. Which of these two kinds of men are you?"

Wendell puts down his goblet, and looks over at Ava, who attempts to hide her terror. Thinking a moment before turning his gaze back to the night man, he says, "*Neither.* And *both.*"

The night man is amused by the answer but continues to try and catch him in his words. "You know, you've been fooled, Mr. Meyers. In the end, it isn't sin or imperfection that keeps a man out of Paradise . . . It's *rebellion.*"

"An odd topic for a casual dinner, don't you think?"

Everyone stops chewing and awaits a reaction from the night man.

"Does this great supper look casual to you, Mr. Meyers?"

Wendell stops chewing as everyone's eyes follow his.

"Perhaps I misspoke. My apologies. I mean, that's a nice apothegm, but I suppose I'm looking for more personalized advice."

That draws a few guarded grins, and a stifled giggle from Ava.

"Well, you didn't let me finish," says the night man, glancing at the girl, whose expression falls grave.

"Sorry. You were saying? *Rebellion?*"

"Yes." He grins. "You, Mr. Meyers, are clearly a *rebel*."

Everyone chuckles in amusement.

"But then," the manager muses with a deep-set smirk, raising a glass, "I suppose we're all rebels here."

They chuckle again, and one gentleman adds a "*Too true.*"

Another, "*Here, here.*"

As the night man takes a drink, his devilish eyes bore into Wendell from across the great spread, and chills run up the back of Wendell's neck.

A tuxedoed waiter with white-gloved hands steps forward and holds out a massive carving knife directly in front of Wendell's face, as if it's on display for him and him alone. He leans back with a start.

"Oh, that's right, where are my manners?" says the night man. "As our esteemed guest this fine evening, Mr. Meyers, would you do us the great honor of carving the beast?"

"Excuse me?" Wendell shakes his head. "I'm no—"

"The main course!" the night man says jubilantly. "The kill. We could all use a bit of protein, don't you think? And someone's got to do the cutting."

Everyone smiles and looks straight at Wendell.

"I don't . . . um, er. Sure, yeah, okay." The cold stares egg him on.

Ava's glare is a little softer than the rest.

With hesitance, he takes the blade from the man, which is even heavier than it looks. It clanks down on the table until he can manage a better grip on the handle.

Several dinner guests mask their reactions at the small mishap.

"It's settled then," says the night man. "Bring out the meat!"

A hush falls over the dinner guests as everyone turns to look out toward one of the doors.

An aureate palanquin, like the ones lifted by slaves carrying princesses emerges from the open doors. It is carried by four waiters by means of two small poles projecting fore and aft. Though small for a covered litter, they carry the ornate box as though it's the Ark of the Covenant, and everyone seems to reverence it as such.

What is this?! is all Wendell can think.

And that predacious stare of the night man, as though the deriving of his own jollies is predicated solely on Wendell's expressions of bewilderment. "Yes," he says. "Good. Set it there, just before our honored guest."

It smells of delicious smoked brisket, seasoned and cooked to perfection. The large, steamy meat tray is set down and pulled out of its lavish container by way of sliding from its house of polished gold. With expert adeptness, the waiters release the contents of the monster and whisk the poles and palanquin away, leaving Wendell only to wonder what species of dead animal gawks back at him through scorched eyes. The size of an adolescent calf, he can't quite tell if it's one part wolf, one part boar, and one part human. The charred creature resembles a roast pig at luau, but it's no pig.

Everyone around the table, including Ava, picks up their own steely knives, and waits for Wendell to do something with his.

They go quiet as they patiently wait, staring.

Wendell only wishes they would return their attention to the appetizers or butter a roll. He takes his fine cloth napkin, and with his left hand, grabs the back of the roast. With his right hand, he grips the carving knife and begins to saw a thick slice from the shoulder of the beast. He drops the tender morsel on a plate, and the plate is passed all the way around to the night man, who bows his thanks. Then Wendell removes the legs, carves off the leg meat, and passes those down the line, a ready waiter providing each empty plate as it is needed. Captivated, everyone watches Wendell's every move, nearly salivating, like some odd, inexplicable scene from the Twilight Zone.

Slowly, everyone begins to converse again, but only in quiet whispers. Wendell carves off the back meat and loins, more off the shoulders and back jowls, almost wrestling the charred monster on the table as he hacks and saws it to pieces. He listens and continues the process, stripping the meat from the animal, until his greasy hands and arms grow tired, and everyone has a generous helping before them.

Small talk is all anyone here can seem to manage. Nothing of use. Nothing of interest. Any talk of the outside world is made with only criticism or guarded derision.

At last, after cutting a small piece from the loin for himself, the waiters quickly take the remains and disappear back into the kitchen, along with the hefty blade. A small sense of relief washes over him. Wendell licks some of the slimy animal fat from his hand and looks down at the moist slab of beef or pork or something other-worldly, which slowly begins to move.

This catches Wendell off guard.

Everyone's portion begins to writhe on their plates, and they pin it ruthlessly. They stab it with their knives, their forks, their nails. The meaty blood and juices splatter and flick about, covering their faces and fine clothing with oily red and brown spots and stains. They jab, and still the slabs move, like flailing fish at the end of each hook. They prick and cut and chew, blood seeping from their lips, down their chins, over teeth, necks, and chests. Even Ava resembles a crazed cannibal, some wild thing that's thrown all traces of class or inhibition or human civility to the chandeliers. Animal juices cover their manicured fingers and hands, and everyone is in a maddened wide-eyed flurry to eat it before it can jump from their dishes. Everyone except Wendell and the night man who watches him carefully. It feels strange, almost as if they are eating a representation of . . . *him*.

The demon revels. "They just can't seem to—"

"Kill it," Wendell interrupts, thinking to himself, *I've never been in the presence of actual cannibals.*

The night man's infuriating smirk grows into a toothy smile, and he chuckles maniacally. That chuckle seems to echo through the walls, through Wendell's own flesh, bouncing around inside his skull. The night man may as well have been a hooded figure wielding a scythe.

He truly is this place, Wendell tells himself, feeling the coarse laughter under his skin.

"We are so glad to have you, Wendell Meyers! *So* glad to have you."

Wendell picks up his dinner knife and stabs the beast flopping around on his own fine china. He cuts off a large morsel and shoves it in his mouth. Chewing it thoroughly, he swallows it down, then looks back at the night man with a newfound confidence. "You know, that's not bad."

19

Chapter Nineteen

Solarin reviews a new file as Lamb looks over a freshly issued warrant and specific related allowances for the forensic excavation of the back of the lot missing in action Earl had led them to. Behind them, a government-contracted bulldozer and a small group of workers wielding jackhammers and concrete chisels set up to begin their work.

Solarin speaks up as he gleans what he needs from the file and to bring Lamb up to speed, "It looks like the property owners of this lot with the newly laid concrete pad are registered as part of a nationwide restaurant and finance chain, Brinkell-Landry Gastronomie International, Inc., or BLG."

Lamb glances up from her papers. "Wasn't their New York branch involved in an investigation a few years ago tied to a money laundering scheme with organized crime?"

Solarin nods, "Yeah, but no indictments were ever issued." He continues with the report, "This is one of the world's leading fine dining establishments and home of a few big-name restaurants and brands. Founded by Roman Brinkell of New York and Ukraine-born, Chicago-raised, Sergei Landry."

"The New York office helped us with the Kenneth Phillips murder," Lamb says. "Perhaps we'll be able to return the favor."

"Depends on what's hiding inside this concrete block," Solarin utters.

"Think we can find a strong enough connection to tie this restaurant juggernaut corporation to Gamble and/or the Gallo family?" Lamb asks.

Solarin shakes his head. "Probably not . . . That camera crew that was following De Luca, the record promoter, who met the mobsters at the same hotel Phillips died in . . . maybe they got some footage that will help connect the dots. BLG has some far-reaching fingers."

"That's a thought," Lamb says, pondering the indirect paper trails, receipts, and witness reports that tied John Whitmore, Kenneth Phillips, and Joseph Gamble to the payola racket. They would need to do another focused sweep to find any links to Brinkell-Landry, as they had already done with the music studios.

"Until all the facts are in, we don't want to bruit around any information," Solarin says. "Spreading reports or rumors can be useful in some instances. This isn't one of them."

Lamb nods.

A whole fleet of suits and lawyers had been unleashed to prevent the excavation and demolition of the concrete pad Lamb and Solarin are set to demolish at any moment, but the DA's office and U.S. federal magistrate judge in cooperation with the FBI's LA field team had already gone through the motions of issuing the needed warrant in record time—*before* the school of bull sharks became any the wiser. Now, however, they foamed at the mouth with cease-and-desist actions in the works.

Finally, the work begins as Lamb and Solarin oversee; the demolition crew couldn't break up the slab fast enough, and hours pass, but Lamb and Solarin hold their ground, watching intently. Hunger be damned, and bathroom breaks, so they tag team it. Neither agent could leave the scene un-supervised. Not until that concrete pad revealed *all* its secrets. They'd been at this case for weeks facing dead-end after dead-end, nearly giving up and closing it down more than once. They would discover Earl's reliability as an eyewitness, and they would prove out the dastardly deeds of these executive millionaires and raise the canopy on the mega-corps involved. After all this time, they would close the file on this, a *finished* case rather than an unsolved mystery.

The bulldozer, jackhammers, and chisels do their work, and the concrete is broken up, excavated, scrutinized piece by piece, until the entire slab is processed and rendered to dust. Eventually, an empty, gaping twelve-by-twelve-foot hole remains where it had been.

"How can it be?" Lamb says, utterly deflated.

Solarin scratches his head, letting out a deep sigh. "I have no words, except maybe a few choice ones for Earl . . . wherever he scurried off to. Their lawyers are going to sink us."

"I thought for sure we'd find them here." Lamb shakes her head, her voice nearly trembling. "The missing pieces, Bianchi, Meyers, enough damning evidence to put Gamble away. I was *sure* we'd find them here."

Solarin puts an arm around her as the demolition crew and forensic analysts consult them for final go ahead on prepping the site for replacement on the federal government's dime, which wouldn't look good on either of their records.

"These things happen," Solarin says as they stroll back to the car. "More often than not, actually."

"What's that?" Lamb asks, "The bad guys getting away with it?"

Solarin thinks a moment. "Yeah."

"Mm-mm. No," she says, unwilling to accept defeat. She stops, turns around, and heads to the job's foreman standing adjacent across the yard. He is a hard and experienced blue-collar man with a respectable presence. Surprised to see her back after their final rendezvous, he turns and straightens.

"Keep digging," she says.

"Agent Lamb," Solarin walks up behind her with a not-so-comforting hand on her shoulder. "Lamb, we can't. The allowances in the warrant are for—"

"I read the warrant," Lamb says, glaring at Solarin, then at the foreman. "Five feet. Give me five more feet."

"If it's not authorized—" the foreman starts.

"I'm authorizing you," Lamb says, wishing they had a cadaver dog.

"It's closing time besides." The foreman shakes his head. "My men have been out here all day."

"So have we. I'll take the heat."

"I'm sorry to say it," the foreman says, "but you don't have the authority."

"That's true. You *don't* have the authority." Solarin acts as second witness.

Lamb's unblinking eyes bore a hole into each of them. "*Five . . . feet.* Give me this. I *know* they're down there. They have to be."

"Earl could have remembered the wrong spot," Solarin says. "I mean the guy's—Look, listen, I want this too, Maggie. I know what it's like on your first big case—"

"*Five . . . feet,*" she says again.

Several uncomfortable moments pass between the three. The foreman relents first. He exhales, sluggishly makes his way over to the bulldozer operator, just out of earshot. The man listens to his superior for a few moments, glances up at Lamb and Solarin, nods, re-enters the bulldozer's cab, and starts up the engine.

Confusion washes over those congregated as the bulldozer commences to dig.

"This is not a wise move," Solarin says. "And this will not look good on our files."

"*My* file," Lamb says.

"*Our* files," he repeats. "I'm letting it happen, aren't I?"

The bulldozer digs and after a while, Lamb whispers, "Thank you."

"Don't thank me until after we're standing in the SAC's office, getting our asses handed to us."

"Fair enough."

Darkness falls, and another 30 minutes later, the bulldozer backs up from the site, and men with flashlights surround the pit.

Lamb and Solarin run up to the edge and peer inside with their own lights.

The multiple rays dance over traces of clothing and body parts mostly buried in the dirt.

Lamb gasps, wide-eyed as horror and relief wash over her simultaneously.

Solarin swallows as they study what's officially become a crime scene. "How many do *you* count?" he asks Lamb as several forensic analysts make their way into the pit near the vicinal bodies.

Lamb huffs. "*Three.*"

"*Me too.*"

"Looks like two males . . . and a female." She shakes her head. "I have

B.C. NAILES

my theories, but who's the girl?" She looks up at Solarin, who looks back at her."

"I don't know. *Poor bastards.*"

* * *

Wendell and Ava stare up at the dark ceiling above them. They both recline in a pile of sheets in a quiet corner of one of the theater's backstage corridors, having just showered together in one of the dressing rooms and made love behind stacks of equipment and set dressing furniture.

"Odd, isn't it?" Ava says, smoking the last vestiges of a cigarette.

"What, my lovemaking?"

"No," she shakes her head listlessly. "This day."

"Oh. Very. I think it's fair to say this has been the oddest day of my life," Wendell says with a smirk. "But in a *good* way."

"Is that so?" Ava rolls over to face him. "Just wait."

"It gets worse?" Wendell raises his eyebrows anxiously.

"Oh yes, and by 'worse' I mean 'better.' I've been with you all night, haven't I?"

"Yes, you have."

"Yes, I have." She giggles as they tickle and play together under black sheets, which were likely theater curtains or wall coverings at some point.

"You're a lucky find, Ava," Wendell says, turning serious.

"A *trouvaille?*" she casually replies in her best French accent.

Wendell nods. "*Oui.*" And they kiss.

They lose themselves in each other's arms for a time until they hear a far-off door open and close.

"Do you think anyone knows we're down here?" Wendell asks, pulling away from her.

"Well, we weren't exactly *silent,* were we?"

Wendell shakes his head and smiles. "Nope."

Ava softly strokes Wendell's forehead and cheek with her titillating fingernails. "*Maybe* someone heard us. Maybe they *watched* us. Maybe they're watching us *now.*"

"Maybe," Wendell says with a guarded smile.

"*Oh, crap!*"

"What's the matter?"

"The show! I've gotta get ready."

"Now? It's got to be the middle of the night."

"Yes, now!" She jumps to her feet, gathers a sheet around her naked body, and makes for her dressing room.

"Tell you what, get dressed, and I'll meet you by the wings in twenty; you can wish me luck."

"Are you kidding?" Wendell says. "My suit's a mess!"

"Oh, right." She pauses, thinking. "Don't worry, I'll find you something. Follow me."

"Perfect."

Wrapped in the buff, she finds Wendell a suit from the costume closet and fetches her own dazzling outfit, passing several other performers as they go. Snickers and gossip follow.

They get changed and hurry over to Ava's station in the backstage green room as several other late-comers shuffle in and join the more prepared dancers who've already made themselves up.

Wendell watches Ava through the mirror of her personal booth, her lovely face framed with small round bulbs as she quickly prepares herself for the stage. He can't help but wonder at the change in everyone's demeanor from the crazed dinner frenzy of animalistic behavior to the current energetic backstage flurry as preparations ensue to the high-brow audience arrivals and after-show that was sure to follow.

"I love performing," Ava says. "Always have. And since we're all prisoners here—"

"What?"

"You know," she says guardedly, "of our own choice."

"Right."

She nods excitedly. "I think dancing requires a sort of shift from your everyday mindset." She begins touching up her foundation. "These pre-show rituals are touchstones—I think they make the transition from regular life to performance more comfortable—Rehearsal brush-ups, stretching, costuming, makeup."

"Yeah, *seems* like loads of fun," he says sarcastically.

She gives him a diminutive look.

"No seriously, thank you for inviting me behind-the-scenes." Wendell notices her disaster area of a desk, cluttered with all sorts of old greasepaint, makeup containers, brushes, empty flower vases, dried flowers, wrappers, clothes, and other accessories. He couldn't function in such a space, but it seems to work for her. "I enjoy seeing what goes on behind the curtain."

"Of course!" she says. "It's fun to have you back here. I can't wait for you to meet my friends, watch me perform. Kind of makes me *nervous*."

"*My* being here? Or the night man's?"

She throws him a dirty glance, sighing ruefully.

Wendell smiles. "No need to be nervous. I'm sure you'll be great."

She moves on to eyeliner and lipstick. "I spent my last four years in a professional dance company. It's weird how the little things help me connect. Then at call time, we head to the wings—which was probably five minutes ago. Did you hear anything?"

"No." Standing behind her, listening to her routine as she prepares, Wendell can't help but adore her even more.

"Sometimes," she continues, "I kinda just sit there at center stage and look up to the lights, out at the audience (or empty seats). I dunno, it helps me transform into character, I guess. Alter my headspace."

"I get that." Wendell puts his hands on her shoulders, and gently massages.

"Mmm." She leans back, enjoying his touch for only a second.

One of the other girls behind them turns up a radio and smiles at them both through Ava's mirror. "*Hi, Ava.*"

"Hey, Tammy. Music is also a big part of our prep," she says. "You hear that?"

Wendell nods, noticing her car keys next to her makeup bag as he listens. "Yeah. Rock. *Classic.*"

She smiles and commences. "I guess it's about that time. You better go find your seat—wouldn't want to upset you-know-who."

"Actually, I would," Wendell says, stepping away from her.

She sits up and watches his reflection in the mirror as he goes. "You did have me worried at dinner."

"I know," he says. "*Me too.* Break a leg."

"Get out of here." She beams like she's in love with him.

If only it were real.

Wendell backs into the shadows where everything is painted black, and winds here and there through back hallways and passages, trying to find the exit to the auditorium. With the help of two stagehands, he makes it out to the seating area, and sees the night man waiting for him in the center of the orchestra section, the best seats in the house. The devil man gestures for Wendell to join him, so he does.

Only for Ava.

It immediately sinks in that sitting next to the night man would be like accompanying his girlfriend's ex-boyfriend to the ballet, though he had a good feeling this wouldn't be Swan Lake.

"She's infatuated with you, you know."

"I wouldn't say that."

"Why not? Did you see her at dinner?"

And every inch of her afterwards. Wendell finds it extremely difficult to look him in the eye.

"She fancies you," says the night man. "Yet you still haven't accepted it."

"What? Accepted what?"

"Think back, Wendell," he says. "*Remember.* Remember the end."

Despite his desire to be obstinate, Wendell's thoughts take him back before his trip . . . before the diner . . . "That morning at *SkyBox?*"

"Yes," he says.

"The lobby by the front doors . . ." Wendell racks his brain. His body doesn't seem to want to remember. ". . . the covered entryway. My disagreement with management. John, Kenneth, Joe. So what? What happened?"

The night man leans in, savoring the conversation. "You know what happened, Wendell. Who else was there? Someone that didn't belong."

"The truck driver . . . whatever he is." *Same guy that punched my lights out on the side of the highway.*

"Yes, but he's not a truck driver, is he?"

Wendell shakes his head. He begins to remember the terrible events that took place *before* he burst through the SkyBox doors onto the LA sidewalk that morning.

"He worked for—"

The night man nods. "Very good. And he's not a truck driver, but he *was* driving a truck."

"Cement." It comes out as a whisper, a traumatic revelation.

"What did they do to you, Wendell, after they dragged you out back?"

Wendell shuts his eyes. He can't accept it. He won't accept it. "Shut up."

The night man smiles and leans back in his comfortable seat. "You're right, Wendell. Too heavy a pre-show topic. Let's just relax. Enjoy the girls, hm?"

Wendell's flashbacks replay between his ears in broken pieces. Tragic, horrific, violent pieces. They render him frozen in his seat. Stuck. Buried. Like a man crushed by concrete.

Members of the orchestra warm up their instruments. The curtain goes up as the music swells. Just what Wendell needs.

Distraction.

The dimly lit, richly decorated set and surroundings introduce a primitive cave flanked by thick, colorful jungle. Six women, dressed in the style of French cabaret, emerge from the dark tunnel dressed as vibrant birds of paradise. A horned demon with black and blue fur emerges from side stage, leaping from an elevated perch on a faux rock waterfall to threaten and face-off against the birds, and after a long and beautiful introductory number, the six part ways—three on each side—to reveal Ava, who emerges in the spotlighted brilliance of center stage in glistening white and silver feathers. Her mere presence raises the lights and frightens the demon away.

The night man glances over at Wendell with a grin, but Wendell doesn't acknowledge him.

Ava then performs as soloist, and Wendell is captivated, believing she is dancing only for him. During her dance, she sees Wendell in the audience, beaming as their eyes lock. This moment, this feeling, for Wendell, is everything he ever wanted out of life. It's all he ever dreamed of. He should be content here. He should want to stay and do this *forever.*

Yet, there is one thing. *Only* one thing he wants more.

After her solo number, and when the entire cast comes out for the

grand spectacle, Wendell stands and exits to his right.

"Bathroom break?" says the night man shallowly as he departs. "*Now? It's not even Act Two.*"

But Wendell knows he knows. Wendell's not making for the restroom. He's not making for his room or backstage to see Ava.

She watches him as she dances, her lighted expression falling dim. And she knows too.

Wendell reaches inside his pocket and grasps Ava's car keys. The keys to her Mercedes. He returns her gaze as he exits the row, and he watches her as he backs slowly up the aisle toward the exit in the back.

Damn, I'll miss you, he thinks to himself.

She stops dancing, and in so doing, stands out even more from the other performers. He lifts a hand, a goodbye, and so does she, but her hand goes to her lips. He disappears behind the back curtains and exits the theater. Swallowing the lump in the back of his throat, he begins to run through the deep crimson hallway padded with carpet on all sides, the draped doorways, the exquisite staircases, the Classical architecture, and high ceilings.

Wendell's heart beats in unison with his flying steps as he seems to float out of the theater gallery and toward the central lobby. Many hotel employees try to stop him and ask questions, but he ignores them.

Wendell runs straight for the exit, down past reception and out through the heavy doors into the arid night. "Mr. Meyers, can we—?"

"No, you can't." Wendell sprints to the garage. That damn garage. But he knows where the Mercedes is parked. *Her* Mercedes. And he knows it will start. It started before. Before he lost her the first time. Pounding the pavement, beating his arms against the cool desert air, he's never moved so fast. Passing a valet who raises an arm, unable to get a word out before Wendell is out of range, he notices the strobing of the lights again, but they can't stop him either. Ghostly drivers sit up from behind their wheels, but they no longer bother him. They can only watch as he tries to make his escape—a most desperate escape—*again.*

Spotting her Mercedes in the same place they had found it parked before, he rattles the keys and opens the door, sitting behind the wheel.

He steals Ava's car, pulls out of the garage, whips around the entry drive, and tears off down the open road. "This place will do anything to keep me here," Wendell huffs with determination, "*then so will I.*"

If anyone or anything stands in his way, they will get hit. These tires would not leave the pavement, not this time. He *would* make it back to Los Angeles. And he *would* have his life back. "*I will,*" he mutters. "I will make it back. I will make it *home.*"

After several miles of driving in the dark, his eyes grow weary, but he shakes if off, re-focusing on the pavement within reach of the headlights.

Out of the blackness he sees Jeanine walking toward him. Her manner is the same as before, only this time it's the middle of the night, and she's lit up. *"JEANINE, MOVE! GET OUT OF THE WAY!"* He honks and nudges the gas pedal even closer to the floor mat. He swerves conspicuously to avoid her or rather for her to avoid him. However, to keep the car on the highway, he's forced to clip her side, and she spins off into the fiery dirt and shrubbery like a rag doll.

"It's not real," he says, hunching. *"That wasn't real."* Still, he peers back at the cloud of dust from both mirrors. *"I hope it's not real."*

"If it's not real . . ." he can hear the night man saying inside his head, *"you can do anything you want."*

Wendell bangs his forehead against the steering wheel until it bleeds, and floors the gas pedal, ripping down the highway at perilous speeds like a bat out of Hell. The Mercedes, pushed to its limits, weaves and groans under the sheer velocity.

Up ahead, a couple walks into his headlights. As they swiftly approach, he recognizes them as his parents. *"Mom?! Dad?!"* Parents he hasn't seen in a very long time. Parents he would have to drive through if he were to escape the Hotel California. Honking the horn, he shouts, *"GET OUT OF THE ROAD!"*

He shakes his head and doubles down, squeezing his eyes shut. *"It's not real. It's not really them. They're in Florida. Where they've always been. They would never leave."*

He lifts his eyelids half a second too early. They look so real. So innocent. And right there, spaced just far enough apart that he'll have to hit and likely kill at least one of them to pass through.

"IT'S . . . NOT . . . REAL!!" Wendell cries out to the moonlit desert sky.

He continues to honk the horn, longer and louder than he did for Jeanine.

"*God, forgive me.*"

20

Chapter Twenty

The morgue's interior is a hapless place, and although it's morning outside, inside breathes a sense of night. The smells are no better than the worst sort of nursing home, and Lamb can barely stomach them. She and Solarin follow a short, stout, balding orderly with dark remnants of hair grasping for dear life onto his shiny pate as the three make their way through a long, white, and dismal hallway, many of its fluorescent lights only teasing a consistent burn.

"Right this way," says the man with nasal tone, turning the corner and leading them down a flight of steps. "It's just down here."

They enter a large, low-ceiling chamber and walk over to a bank of refrigerated body drawers. The orderly examines the numbers on his clipboard against those on each designated drawer, then pulls out the three corresponding bodies on their respective trays.

He double checks his names and numbers, then steps back, allowing Lamb and Solarin a clear view of all three bodies.

The officers stand looking at the corpses, two of which they recognize from photos in their files, and from the pit the previous evening: *Wendell Meyers* and *Jeremy Bianchi*. The third, *Jeanine Margaret Tomlinson*—a close friend of Wendell Meyers, according to a few of his co-workers at SkyBox.

Solarin leans close to study her face as Lamb moves around to the other side of the drawer.

"Jeanine," she says softly.

"Mm-hm." Solarin steps over to examine the corpses of Meyers and Bianchi, and Lamb joins him.

The orderly wanders across the room, attending to other business, giving them some privacy.

Confirming the orderly is out of earshot, Solarin turns to Lamb. "So."

Lamb sighs. "So."

"Gamble was playing both sides," Solarin says.

"It would appear."

"A *dangerous* approach. I have to admit, I'm a little surprised he's still above ground. Mobsters, labels, hitmen, and businessmen, with Joe smack dab in the middle. I'm afraid he's going to make his obscenely expensive counsel earn their inflated rates."

Lamb nods. "Depending on forensics, he could still burn for this."

"True. Not many places left to hide. He's running the payola scandal, using the mob to push his clients, make the necessary threats while using his SkyBox team to pay off who he needs to and then cook the books, move some investments around, cover the trails, distance himself from the action—which is where Meyers and Bianchi here come in."

Lamb picks it up, "Without taking his partners morality into account."

"Or his employees," Solarin says. "As I see it, Meyers and Bianchi went first. *'Bury 'em out back—I know a concrete guy.'*"

"Right," Lamb says, "Then Whitmore and Phillips start to feel a little guilty, a little uncomfortable, 'cause now they've got blood on their hands. They too start to question their involvement with the mob, Brinkell-Landry."

"Guilt by association," Lamb says. "Now it's gone way beyond payola, fraud, and money laundering."

"So Gamble's a nihilist, a schemer, and everyone else pays for it." Solarin shakes his head with a subdued but righteous indignation.

"Well, the others aren't *completely* innocent, are they?"

"Jeanine, perhaps." Solarin glances back at her reclining corpse. "Seems all she did was make friends with the wrong accountant."

"Wrong place, wrong time," Lambs says, sounding perfectly cliché.

"Looks that way."

"Well, one thing's for sure," Lamb says, "and it hasn't changed since we picked him up."

"What's that?" Solarin says.

"Gamble is a son-of-a-bitch."

Solarin nods. "Can't be called the City of Angels . . . without exposing a few demons."

"Gamble's ties to the restaurant chain who owns the property will be hard for the lawyers to ignore . . ." Lamb says.

They both take a few more moments with the bodies, then nod to the orderly from across the room as they exit.

"We're all done here," Solarin says.

Lamb finishes her thought: ". . . And the dead speak louder than the living."

"That's for the jury—They'll have our reports."

* * *

Los Angeles is just how Wendell left it. He pulls Ava's Mercedes over to the curb across the street from his luxury flat in Cheviot Hills, one of the nicer residential areas of town. He peers out at the front steps of his high-rise studio apartment, blood and old tears still caking his face. He can't believe he's made it back; he takes his time, savoring the familiar street scene.

Lowering his head onto the steering wheel, he sobs. *I just mowed down the only people that ever really cared for me. So many sins—likely three counts of manslaughter. But it's not real! And I had to get away!*

"It's . . . not . . . real." But his weeping does little to bring him comfort. His shed tears may as well have been the tens of thousands of dollars he wasted on a selfish life.

When the waterworks run out, he turns to watching his neighbors go about their mundane daily routines; the elderly European woman across the street fetches her mail in a pink bath robe and curlers; the studio man pulls out of his basement garage in his convertible and heads to work; the mom takes her boys to daycare in a double-stroller; the fitness model twins jog by, avoiding eye contact with anyone; old 'geriatrics' lets out his cats.

"Nothing's changed," Wendell mutters, dried tears obscuring his vision only slightly.

He gets out of the car, and manually opens his garage door. Pulling Ava's ride inside, he closes the garage, and saunters up the steps to his flat. His shame almost unbearable, he enters and strolls over the familiar avocado-green carpet to his roomy bed chamber. He spins on his heel, raising his arms, more out of grief or asking divine forgiveness than elation from having escaped the desert prison. He lets out an extended sigh and allows himself to fall backward onto his oh-so-comfortable bedspread. "I'm home. Finally . . . *home.*"

He almost closes his eyes, but for fear of waking somewhere else, he holds his lids unnaturally wide. He would stay awake as long as possible.

"Don't go to sleep," he whispers, as though it's an affirmation. *"Don't . . . fall asleep."*

So he just lies there and stares up at the ceiling, hungry, tired, and alone, but without the energy to do anything about it.

He suddenly comes alert to a rattling at the front door downstairs. Keys in the doorknob.

That was close.

He pops his head up from the pillow and listens. Someone is inside his apartment. *Several* people. He can hear them talking. Their footsteps in the entryway move past his home office and toward the kitchen. They walk around underneath him on the main floor. Could it be thieves? Squatters? Are they robbing the place?

Wendell jumps out of his bed and realizes this would be an opportune time to fetch a gun . . . if only he had one.

He creeps down the stairs to discover a middle-aged woman in upright business attire. She clasps a real-estate brochure to her chest and proceeds to give a tour of the house to a young couple.

"What the hell?!" Wendell rushes down the remaining steps to confront the woman. "This is my house. Who are you? What do you think you're doing?"

The three completely ignore him, as though he's not even there.

"This is the dining area," says the woman, gesturing at the dinner table and island bar. "Very spacious, as you can see. Plenty of natural light.

Right outside, there's a lovely veranda and lounging area. Two-car garage and mini wine cellar in the basement."

The couple wander around attentively as though they're selecting items for a wedding registry, his arm around her back, and carefree smiles on both of their faces. Wendell stomps forward with a few ready expletives to dish out, but notices the young woman's protruding belly, and rethinks his words.

"Excuse me . . . *Excuse me! HEY! This is my house!*"

"Did you say there are two bedrooms upstairs?" asks the young man.

"That's correct," says the woman, who must be their real estate agent. "Would you like to see?"

"Sure," the young man says.

With bravado, Wendell steps in front of the pretentious woman, and stares her down, but she avoids eye contact, and walks straight for him.

He holds up his hands to stop her by the shoulders, and she walks right through him.

Wendell reels, and the pregnant young woman also passes by under his chin. He finds himself on the floor, watching helplessly as they saunter up the stairwell, utterly unaware of his presence.

"No," he mutters, dropping his head low, unwilling to accept the reality. All along, he had thought the Hotel California, with its whispering ghosts, its excesses, luxuries, and sweet debaucheries, was the dream. That Ava was the dream. But here, alone, now, trapped on the wrong side of the mortal veil, he realizes—this is the dream. His swimming psyche suddenly reaches to fill in the gaps of everything that transpired before his fateful journey east over that bleak western desert. He suddenly remembers the stark reality of his feud with the partners, the brutality of being shot and dragged to the back of the lot and beat to a pulp, and the finality of being dropped in the pit, right next to the cold dead bodies of Jeanine and Jeremy. The trauma flashes through his mind like quickly cut scenes from old horror films, his tears and mucus spilling over that avocado carpet while he wonders if he was or is even here at all. A deep-set wish for vengeance begins to surface but is almost instantly squelched by the mere thought of his own captivity.

"That was it," he sobs. *"This is all there is . . . God, help me."*

Like a distant echo, he can hear the night man laughing. "How impetuous you've been, Wendell Meyers. What did you think would happen? I told you you could never leave. Come, let us bring you some more wine. What vintage? Perhaps something post-1969?"

The demoralizing image of Ava crumpled on the floor weeping next to her dressing room mirror plagues him. Other performers try to comfort her, and she stands and fades into the dark on the arms of two of her pool party pretty boys.

"I love you, Ava," he wants to tell her, *"And I'm sorry. I'm sorry for leaving."* But he doesn't know if she'll ever give him the chance to apologize.

Leo, too, wanders into his thoughts, welcome or not, like it's the first day they met. "Don't worry, Wendell. We have all the time in the world to get better acquainted. And I'll be sure to introduce you to my family when they arrive. Care to take a trip?"

"No," Wendell says. "No, no, no, no, *NO!*"

Wendell continues to sob. No matter where he goes, he's trapped. *Utterly* trapped. He can't stop the voices in his head. He can't unsee the images of the dead. All those people that checked into the Hotel California over the years. He knows he's losing it, but he can't get out.

Several minutes later, the young couple and the real estate agent wander back down the stairs. They pass by him again, but now he's curled up against the back of the couch, outside their walking path. They walk through the living room and head out to see the garage, the storage space, and the basement with its wine cellar. After they see what they came to see, they finally leave, locking the door behind them.

"Welcome," Wendell whispers mockingly. *"Welcome to—"*

He stands, composes himself, wiping away his tears and blood streaks, and he slowly shuffles up the stairs to his bedroom. He climbs over the sheets and lies down on his back, gently relaxing his sore muscles and closing his eyes. He rests there for hours, meditating, calming himself, coming to terms with his situation until he's finally able to fall asleep.

21

Chapter Twenty-One

The desert. The open road. *Freedom*. Maggie Lamb and her friend, Jon—who she met at the dusky late-night bar—cruise the open highway, oblivious to any speed limit or safety precaution. The wind whips Lamb's hair from the open driver's side window. Alternative rock music softly resonates under their casual conversation.

"So what made you decide to leave the bureau?" Jon asks.

Maggie thinks about the question. "I don't know."

"You know, a lot of people get trapped in LA," he says. "The movies. The music scene. They come out for the glitz, glamor, sunny beaches. But pretty soon, they get caught up in the darker side of Hollywood—readily apparent at the wild parties, pursuits of pleasure, self-indulgence. They get seduced by its allure, and then realize it's all an illusion. A farse. Only after it's too late."

"Is that what happened to you? Is that why you're still out there?"

Jon stares out the window. "I think I recognized it for what it was out of the gate. When I first moved to LA, my employer invited my buddy and I to a company party on the Boulevard . . . DJ, drinks, neon lights. We were lovin' it. Not an hour in, these two girls—they could have been *high-end* Vegas escorts, I mean—anyway, they come over and sit down, practically on our laps, and start flirting with us. And we think we struck the jackpot. Anyway, after a bit, they take us up to a bedroom and start getting frisky, like they're drunk and about to strip—and I guarantee they thought we were more buzzed than we actually were. I'm thinking we're gonna get lucky, so I glance around to make sure we're alone, and that's when I see the surveillance cameras in the upper corner of the room and open closet, partially obscured by a mural and the closet door, red lights blinking."

"Your boss wanted blackmail material," Lamb says with a smile.

Jon nods, "Too good to be true. I grabbed my friend, and we were out of there."

"At least they didn't drug you," Lamb says.

"Their looks were enough."

"So that's LA, huh?"

"That's LA."

"You still haven't told me why you stayed."

"I'm leaving right now, aren't I? With you?"

Lamb gives him a sidelong glare. "For good? Come on."

"You still haven't told me why you left the bureau."

Again, Maggie contemplates the question. "I guess it was Solarin."

"Your partner?"

"Yeah. He's a good guy. One of the best. And I saw what the job did to him. I mean, don't get me wrong, he's still a great guy, but . . ."

After a moment, Jon asks, "But what?"

She glances at him from behind the wheel. "It was his eyes, I think. The light had gone from his eyes. It would briefly spark when his daughters were around, but then it would vanish again."

"Interesting."

Lamb shrugs. "And . . . it's a heavy job. A . . . *heavy* . . . job."

"Of course."

"And I'm not a cynic," she says.

"Only a cynic would say that," Jon replies.

They smile.

Lamb watches the horizon, which doesn't change. The sparse vegetation and endless desert. The airstream and outside heat battle it out. Eventually, the desert highway cools down. The comfortable seats start to lose their comfort. Lamb checks her gas gauge. Half a tank. *Not to worry,* she thinks to herself. *Something will come up.*

She regrets leaving Solarin; she truly enjoyed working with him, respected him, and looked up to him. Whether her future included law enforcement or something completely different, she would try to emulate his calm and cool approach to life. His morals. His loving attitude toward family and country and duty. His kindness, notwithstanding that sharp intelligence.

"What are you thinking about?" Jon asks.

She gives him a glance. "Oh, nothing."

Up ahead at a great distance against the graying blue sky, something stands out. A tiny spot of color against the vast, light brown backdrop. Lamb squints for a sharper view. "What is that?"

"What?" Jon asks.

"Up there. Just ahead."

Jon shifts in his seat and leans forward, wiping his eyes for a better look. "Don't know."

More details become visible as they approach.

"It's a hotel," Lamb says. *"Or . . . used to be."*

It gets bigger, closer. The spot of color becomes many. A building appears.

A sun-wrecked, broken-down sign too takes shape just off the highway, likely unlit for decades. Lamb can't quite make out the broken words. They pass the sign, and immediately see what it advertises. A long-abandoned stop-off in the desert. The only thing around. For miles and miles. Like a haunting mirage, a broken shell of a once luxurious retreat.

Her curiosity overtaking her, she pulls off the highway into the long sand-covered entry drive, badly cracked and overgrown with mature weeds and sagebrush.

"What are you doing?" asks Jon, surprised at the detour.

"Just taking a quick break to stretch my legs," Lamb says playfully. "I mean, look at this place."

Jon looks up at the wilting palms, the broken windows and doors, and the eerie darkness inside them. "I'm looking at it—kind of freaks me out."

"Fascinating," Lamb says, in awe of its size and undeniable presence, despite its poor location and upkeep. She peers upward and sees the remnants of the building's dilapidated masthead. *"Hotel California,"* she

Hotel
California
E.C. NAILES

mutters.

"Strange," Jon says. "I've never heard of it."

"Neither have I," Lamb says, exiting the car and studying the building more closely. She slowly walks toward the front doors, long felled from their hinges, and faded from their aureate finish. It reminds her of an old hotel in Atlanta from her childhood, or what was left of it. It had been thirty years since it burned down. They had since tried to rebuild it three times, but funding fell through, there were accidents, faulty machinery. And there it sat, haunting her throughout her childhood and on through adulthood.

Up in one of the windows of the fourteenth floor, she sees the form of something . . . or *someone.*

"Wh—?"

She focuses on the figure. A man or— "What the hell is that?" she says.

"What?" Jon asks. "What are you looking at?"

Lamb takes another step forward and as she does, another figure appears; the ghostly reflection of a woman stepping up behind the lone man. She wraps one arm around his shoulder, and both figures stand there in the window watching her from fourteen stories up.

"I'll be damned," she mutters.

"What do you see?" Jon asks.

She looks back at Jon, then points up toward the window, but no one is there, only the same empty darkness that appears behind the dozens of other broken windows on the building's weather-worn facade. Lamb's hand goes to cover her mouth, and the investigative detective comes out. She hurries forward to enter the building.

"HEY!" Jon yells from behind, stopping her. "What are you doing? We're in the middle of nowhere. We've got to hit the road, find a gas station."

Lamb looks up at the window again. She could swear she recognized the man as *Wendell Meyers,* the same man whose corpse occupied the body tray between Jeanine Tomlinson and Jeremy Bianchi at the morgue weeks ago.

She shakes her head.

Couldn't be. He was dead and buried . . . properly.

She swallows, and starts to walk backwards, keeping her eyes on that window.

"You're right," she says softly.

"What?" Jon says.

She clears her throat, turning toward him. "You're right. We need to keep moving."

She passes Jon, bumping his shoulder, and gets back in the car.

Jon nods, confused, then joins her.

Lamb stares at the building's dismal frontage once more before putting the car in reverse and backing toward the highway.

They pull up to a gas station fifteen miles down the road from the hotel, but they get out of the car and discover it to be derelict, abandoned, and without working pumps.

"Let me drive," Jon says.

"Sure." Lamb throws him the keys, and they get back in their seats. "What do you want to do?"

He starts the ignition. "Let's hope we've got enough in the tank to get us to the next town."

They pull out onto the highway and drive off over the dark desert horizon.

"What *is* the next town?" Lamb asks.

"Who the hell knows?"

END

B.C. HAILES

About the Author/Artist

Brian Charles Hailes is the award-winning writer/illustrator of four graphic novels entitled *Avila, Blink, Dragon's Gait,* and *Devil's Triangle,* the children's picture books *Tryp, Skeleton Play,* and *Don't Go Near the Crocodile Ponds.* Other titles he has illustrated include *Heroic: Tales of the Extraordinary, Passion & Spirit: The Dance Quote Book, Continuum* (Arcana Studios), as well as *McKenna, McKenna, Ready to Fly,* and *Grace & Sylvie: A Recipe for Family* (American Girl). In addition to his several publishing credits, Hailes has also illustrated an extensive collection of fantasy, science fiction, comics, and children's book covers as well as interior magazine illustrations.

Hailes has received numerous awards for his art from across the country, including Winner of the L. Ron Hubbard Illustrators of the Future contest out of Hollywood. His artwork has also been featured in the 2017-2023 editions of Infected By Art.

Hailes studied illustration, graphic design, and creative writing at Utah State University where he received his Bachelor of Fine Arts (BFA) degree, as well as the Academy of Art University in San Francisco. He has been a regular panelist and presenter at Salt Lake Comic Con, FanX, and LTUE, where he was the Artist Guest of Honor in 2022, as well as Artist GOH at Conduit 2013. He has also appeared as a special guest at San Diego Comic Con, and is currently an official judge for the Illustrators of the Future contest.

Hailes currently lives in Salt Lake City with his wife and four boys, where he continues to write, paint and draw regularly. More of his work can be seen at:

HailesArt.com
DrawItWithMe.com
Instagram: drawitwithmeofficial
Facebook: drawitwithme
ArtStation: bchailes

An Illustrated Science Fiction Novel
AVILA
HAILES DEFEND!
COMING SOON!

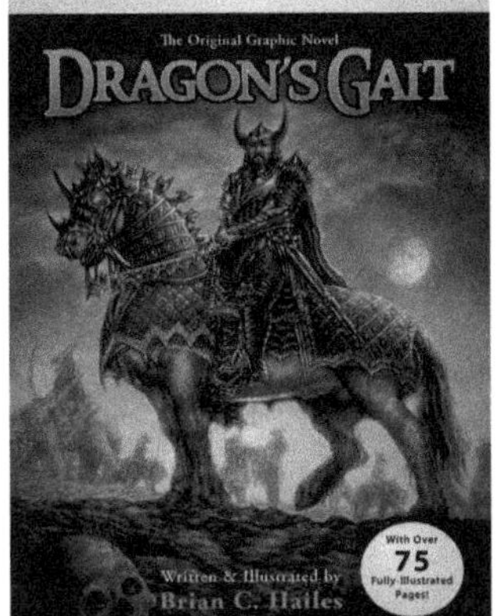

The Original Graphic Novel
DRAGON'S GAIT
With Over 75 Fully-Illustrated Pages!
Written & Illustrated by Brian C. Hailes

KAMIKAZI
BRIAN C HAILES
JOHN ENGLISH

DRAW IT WITH ME: THE
DYNAMIC
FEMALE FIGURE
BRIAN C HAILES

DRAW IT WITH ME A
STUDY OF THE
HUMAN FORM
With Over 500 Sketches, Gestures & Anatomy of the Male & Female Figure
BRIAN C HAILES

DRAW IT WITH ME: THE
ELEGANT
FEMALE FORM
BRIAN C HAILES

COLOR MY OWN
HALLOWEEN STORY
AN IMMERSIVE, CUSTOMIZABLE
COLORING BOOK
FOR KIDS (THAT RHYMES!)
by BRIAN C HAILES

COLOR MY OWN
Fairy Story
AN IMMERSIVE, CUSTOMIZABLE
Coloring Book
FOR KIDS (THAT RHYMES!)
By BRIAN C HAILES

COLOR MY OWN
Princess Story
AN IMMERSIVE, CUSTOMIZABLE
Coloring Book
FOR KIDS

IF I WERE A
SPACEMAN
A RHYMING ADVENTURE THROUGH THE COSMOS
BRIAN C HAILES
ILLUSTRATIONS BY RTH LUADTHONG

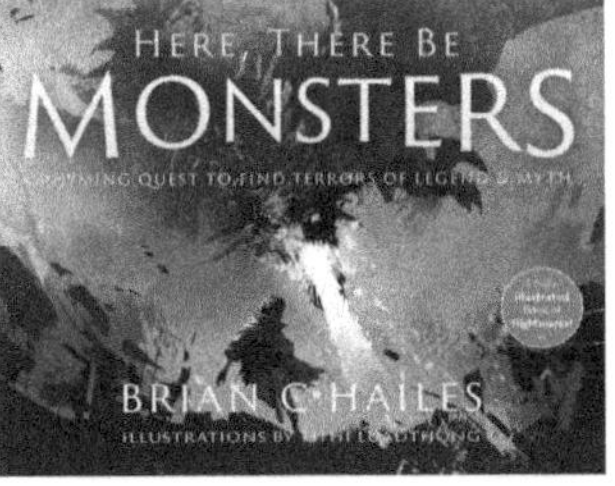

HERE, THERE BE
MONSTERS
A RHYMING QUEST TO FIND TERRORS OF LEGEND & MYTH
BRIAN C HAILES
ILLUSTRATIONS BY RTH LUADTHONG

Can We Be Friends?
STORY BY EDIE NEW
ART BY CINDY HAILES